THE POWER OF PEGASUS

By Milush Black

This novel is entirely fiction. The names, characters and incidents portrayed in it are the work of the author's imagination. Any resemblance to actual persons, living or dead, events or localities is entirely coincidental.

ISBN: 978 1 7384817 0 5

DEDICATION

For Maya Elisabeth Bornhauser, a loving, kind woman and mother.

CONTENTS

ACKNOWLEDGMENTS

I wish to thank all the people who inspired me to write this story. In my life, I met many people who made it evident how important is to stand up for human rights and to fight against bullying and abuse. I wish to thank my family, which always has been supportive of me, and express my gratitude to the human rights activists, lawyers and journalists who report the truth, while risking that their phone might be infected with Pegasus. I am grateful to the people in Bahrain and the United Arab Emirates who stand up against oppression, while exposing themselves to danger. You are so brave. My heart goes out to you.

CHAPTER 1

All of a sudden, the music on my iPhone started playing. I trembled, for I hadn't touched the phone at all. I didn't know what was happening. Was my phone faulty? Did someone or something have control over it? I took the phone, restarted it, and put it on my bed. I went to the other side of my room and watched it. The iTunes app opened again, and the song "Stop" by Jamelia began to play. Was it possible that Mo had hacked my phone? Or had I simply lost my mind?

One year ago, I was smoking outside my house when I received an anticipated call.

"Hello," I said.

"Hi, Sophie. It's William from TopTech people. Good news. I just heard back from CooperateEvent. They would like to offer you the job. The salary they are willing to pay is twenty-eight thousand pounds per annum. How does that sound to you? Do you need to think about it?"

"Let me think about it," I replied, then waited a few seconds for effect.

"OK, I thought about it. I will take the job."

William laughed. My start in London had been tough, for I had been working behind the bar just to struggle to pay the rent for a single room. This offer was, therefore, kind of a lifesaver.

"Great, congratulations again. So well done. I will let them know. They will send you the contract via email," William responded.

I thanked William, wished him a lovely day, and hung up the phone. Although the job offer was good news, I had a weird feeling about it. "It must be the disappointment," I thought. I was a graphic designer, and this position would not involve any creative tasks. Naturally, I had dreamed of finding employment that would have enabled me to live up to my artistic potential. I called my father and told him the good news.

"Yes, great," he replied.

His tone of voice had been very unpleasant, as usual. He had not even congratulated me, so I ended the conversation quickly.

On my first day of employment, I was very apprehensive.

I had always been a bit anxious going into a new environment, for I was afraid that the others wouldn't approve of me. This fear had been my companion since I had been bullied as a child. To feel as confident as possible, I did my best to dress smart. I chose a black long sleeve, blue jeans, a green blazer, and black fake leather boots. My clothes weren't of good quality. Especially my shoes. I liked real leather boots but couldn't afford them.

My reflection in the mirror was pleasing, although I wasn't a beauty queen. I was a tall, skinny girl with hazel-brown eyes and red-brown hair.

As I never ate breakfast, I was on my way to Oxford Circus ten minutes later. I lived close to Finsbury Park station, which was convenient because I didn't have to change the tube. The underground was very crowded that morning. Therefore, I was very relieved when I finally got out. On the way to the office, I went to Starbucks to get myself a soya cappuccino to pass the time, for I was a bit early. Ten minutes later, I entered the building and took the elevator. Just a couple of seconds after I had stepped into the office, a woman with short brown hair came walking towards me.

"You must be Sophie. I am Margaret. The HR."

Her tone of voice was really friendly, which I found encouraging.

"Hi, nice to meet you."

"Did you have a long journey?" she asked.

"No, I took the Victoria line from Finsbury Park. It only took me twenty minutes to get here."

"That's fantastic. Please follow me. I will show you to your desk."

Just as I had taken my seat, a black, athletic build guy approached us.

"Sophie, this is Vince. He is our IT guy. He will give you your laptop and set it up for you," Margaret said.

"Hi, Vince. Nice to meet you."

"Likewise, Sophie. Welcome to the team," he replied.

"Sophie, you will have your first online meeting in one hour, and at lunch, you and I will go to a restaurant. We always do this on the first day to treat the new starters," Margaret said.

This was most welcome, for I wouldn't have to pay for my lunch.

"Sounds great. I look forward to it."

Margaret left, and I felt rather foolish sitting at my desk without having anything to do while Vince was busy installing all the applications. One hour later, I had an introduction meeting with my team, which worked abroad. They all seemed very nice, but I became more and more aware that this job wouldn't involve any creativity at all. I was so disappointed and tried to hide it as well as possible. At lunch, Margaret and I went to a Thai restaurant. We both ordered Pad Thai, which was very delicious. We had the usual small talk and then returned to the office. Shortly after lunch, Margaret emailed the entire company, informing them that I had just started and encouraged the others to introduce themselves to me.

At about three in the afternoon, I went out for a cigarette. Just when I had re-entered the office, an Arab-looking guy came walking towards me.

"Hi, you must be Sophie, the new starter," he said.

He was tall and had black curls. He wasn't exactly my type, but he wasn't ugly either. His skin had a very nice tint, which I found appealing. Everything in his manners demonstrated a lot of confidence.

"Hi, nice to meet you. What is your name?"

"Mohamed, but everyone calls me Mo."

The gaze he gave me exhibited a certain curiosity.

"Where are you from?" I inquired.

"I am from Bahrain. It's an island close to the United Arab Emirates. I would say we are way more liberal there. Where are you from?"

"I am from Switzerland."

This information was certainly intriguing to him, for he had a huge smile and a twinkle in his eyes.

"Oh, what a beautiful, rich country."

"Yeah, it is," I replied.

The conversation itself was nothing but the usual small talk and, therefore, of little interest, but Mo's confidence was intriguing to some degree. The reason for that was, of course, my own insecurity.

"Well, welcome to the team. I will talk to you later," he said.

I went back to my desk and began to read my emails, which contained the new-starter information. Later in the evening, I was approached by a handsome-looking guy.

"Hi, Sophie. How is your first day going?"

"It's very intense, as I have been given lots of information. What is your name?"

"Dylan, I am the senior manager. Don't you remember? We had the interview together."

I was mortified. I had just seen him once before in a Zoom interview.

"Oh, my god. I didn't recognise you. You look different in real life," I replied.

He seemed to find that amusing.

"It doesn't surprise me. I was really casually dressed when we had the call and didn't have my glasses on. How are you finding it so far?"

It was a huge relief that he wasn't offended.

"I like it," I said, which was a total lie.

"Oh, good. The first week can be very demanding, but you will see that you will love it here."

At the end of the day, I walked past Mo and waved at him to say goodbye. He appeared to be surprised by it and didn't wave back. I found that peculiar, for he had appeared to be such an open and unreserved person in the afternoon. On the way home, I got myself two gin and tonic cans, something I had never done before as I had never been much of a drinker. Back in my room, I actually talked to myself and said, "I hate this job."

CHAPTER 2

The following day, a plumb but very kind-looking employee of CooperateEvent approached me.

"Hi, Sophie. My name is Sebastian. How was your first day?"

"It was good. There is a lot to learn, but I like it," I replied.

"I am glad. It must be weird, though, that your entire team works abroad," he said.

"Honestly, I really don't mind."

"That's good. We are very social here, and you will always find someone to talk to if you feel lonely. Do you want to join us for lunch later?"

Large groups always made me feel apprehensive, so I wasn't eager to join him and his friends. However, I felt obliged to accept the invitation, for I didn't wish to offend him.

“Sure, I would love to,” I replied.

“Great, we are going at half past twelve. I will find you then.”

“See you then,” I replied with a smile to pretend that I was happy about the invitation.

We were accompanied by two girls who appeared to be rather stiff. I usually preferred the company of open-minded, down-to-earth people. Therefore, I wasn’t entirely sure if I would fit into that group. On the way to the restaurant, we passed a very handsome stranger. He was tall and had dark brown hair and blue eyes. He wore a grey jacket and blue jeans. His physical appearance was hypnotising. My companions greeted him, but he didn’t respond. He only stared at me. I was mesmerised by the gaze he had given me. My conversations with others didn’t appeal to me, for I had never been a fan of small talk. I wanted to ask how they were acquainted with the handsome man, but I resisted the temptation.

The mystery, however, was solved as soon as we returned to the office. He was working for CooperateEvent as well. He was seated at a desk close to the entrance. I couldn’t believe that I had never noticed him before. The workplace had instantly become a lot more interesting. I considered it unwise to reveal that I was infatuated with him, so I suppressed a smile. Later in the afternoon, the handsome guy approached Dylan, who was sitting not far away from me. I felt my heart skip a beat and found it hard to concentrate.

"Dylan, do you know when the reports will be finished?" he asked.

"I do not know. The reports are not my responsibility."

"Oh, OK then."

He was staring at me when he passed my desk. Once he was out of sight, I grinned. Although I was lacking in confidence, I had the suspicion that he had only sought a conversation with Dylan to be able to look at me again.

The following day, I went out for a cigarette at about three in the afternoon. I saw two girls standing outside, whom I had seen in the office before. Both of them were short and curvy. One looked like she could have been from India, and the other had strawberry-blonde hair and blue eyes. I approached them.

"Hi, do you work for CooperateEvent as well?" I asked.

"Yes," the strawberry-blonde girl replied.

Her tone of voice had been rude. I immediately started to feel uncomfortable.

"What is your name?" the Indian-looking girl asked.

"Sophie, and yours?" I replied.

"My name is Sita, and this is Brigitta."

The girl called Brigitta looked very annoyed.

"Nice to meet you," I replied.

Suddenly, I felt resentful to have a further conversation with them, but I thought that some small talk was required of me.

"How do you like working for CooperateEvent?" I asked.

"It's good. I like it," Sita replied.

Brigitta didn't answer. She looked like she had just swallowed a lemon. Her appearance was indeed very unpleasant. She wasn't pretty, and her facial expression and her unfriendly behaviour gave me a strong desire to keep my distance from her. She reminded me of one of those angry little dogs that barked at everyone and bit anyone who came too close to them.

"Great, do you have any plans for the weekend?" I asked.

"We may go to the cinema tomorrow. The rest of the weekend, probably nothing. Do you have any plans?" Sita asked.

"No, I haven't got anything planned yet. It's kind of tight with money, as I just started working. So I will probably stay at home and hang with my housemate."

I instantly regretted mentioning my financial situation. It was obvious that Brigitta found it shameful that someone couldn't afford to go out. Shortly after returning to the office, I heard Brigitta's voice. She sounded hysterical.

"Are you going to talk to her now or not?" she shrieked.

"No, she is busy right now. I will talk to her when she is free," I heard Mo respond, in a calm voice.

I had no idea what this conversation had been about and didn't give it much thought, but I had the suspicion that there was something seriously wrong with Brigitta. I didn't want that girl close to me in any way, and I swore to myself that I would do my best to avoid her. The next day, at about two in the afternoon, Mo came to my desk.

"Hi, how are you doing?" he asked.

"I am good, thanks. How are you?"

"Really good. Almost weekend. Some of us are going for coffee. Do you like coffee?"

"Yeah, I love coffee. I can't live without it," I replied.

"Would you like to join us?" he asked.

"I already had my lunch break, and I have a meeting soon. I can't."

He looked disappointed.

"No?" he asked.

"No," I replied. "Another time, I would love to."

This wasn't entirely truthful. Mo appeared to be very chatty. I liked that because I enjoyed being around people who were leading the conversation, but apart from that, I wasn't very eager to talk to him. I couldn't say exactly why. Maybe because he appeared to be untrustworthy to me.

"Another time then," he replied.

On Friday, Mo initiated a conversation with me again while I stood in the kitchen.

"Do you have any plans for the weekend?" he asked.

"Yeah, I do. I go out," I replied.

As a matter of fact, I didn't have any plans for the weekend. I had lied to him because I had been worried that he might have asked me out if I would have been honest with him.

"Oh, really? What are you going to do?"

"Probably go out drinking," I replied.

"Oh, drinking is the best. What do you drink when you go out?"

"Gin and tonic."

"I drink gin and tonic, too," Mo said.

I wasn't sure why he kept following me around, but it wasn't welcome at all. Mo appeared to be the kind of person who told people what they wanted to hear to win their approval. Some people appreciated that, but I considered it deceitful.

"Nice. Well, I have to go now. Have a nice weekend," I said.

He was standing very close to me, making me think he lacked boundaries or didn't respect mine.

"Oh, you have to go already?" he asked.

"Yes, unfortunately."

"OK, have a nice weekend," Mo said.

I was relieved that I had survived my first week. On the way home, I bought myself about five gin and tonic cans to drown out my frustration. In the kitchen, I met my Sri Lankan housemate, Asiri. He was a really nice person. I didn't really have friends in London, and therefore, I was always glad when I could talk to him.

"You are drinking," Asiri noticed, for he had never seen me drink alcohol before.

"Yeah, it's Friday. I just need something to relax," I replied.

"How was your first week? Do you like it?" he asked.

"No, not really. I am a graphic designer, and this job isn't creative at all."

"It's hard when you start. Maybe you will enjoy it later."

"Yeah, maybe," I replied, although I very much doubted it. "How was your week?" I asked.

"Normal. You know, as an accountant, it is always the same. Counting money."

It sounded very boring to me.

"Are you happy with your job?" I asked.

"It's alright. I would prefer to work in a bank. I would earn more money."

"This is understandable. Life is so tough after graduation. I thought I would get my dream job as a graphic designer right away, but the reality is so different."

He smiled. I guessed that he thought that I was a bit naïve.

"Most people have to work a long time until they find a job that they really like," Asiri replied.

He was right, of course, but I didn't like it. I wished him a lovely evening and went out for a cigarette. "My job is so boring, and my social life is non-existent. I earn more than I did behind the bar, but I am still just able to afford a small room in a shared house," I thought while smoking. To distract myself from my gloomy sentiments, I spent the rest of the weekend fantasising about the handsome guy from the office.

On Monday, I went out for lunch by myself. On my way back to the office, I crossed paths with my crush. He didn't say anything. He just stared at me again. I asked myself if he would ever introduce himself to me. On Friday, late in the afternoon, I went out for a smoke, where I encountered Mo in the company of a short black guy. I went over to them, as it would have been impolite not to do so.

"Hi, Sophie. How are you?" Mo asked.

"I am good. How are you?" I replied.

"I am good. I'm super happy it is soon the weekend. This is Rhys, by the way."

Rhys shook my hand.

"How do you like your job?" Rhys asked.

"It's OK, but I feel that I don't really fulfil my potential here. It's a lot just copy and paste," I replied.

"The potential is something really hard to reach," Mo declared.

Rhys nodded to agree with Mo.

"True, but if you don't try, you will never really be happy. So you kind of have a responsibility to do your best. If you don't, you will always regret it," I said.

"Mo, open the gate for me."

We all turned our heads. There he was, my crush. He was wearing his grey jacket again and had a pack of beers in his hand.

"Achh, excuse me, Sophie," Mo said.

He went over to the gate and opened it. Both Mo and the handsome guy came back to us. I felt the sweat on my hands and my heart beating inside my chest.

"Hi, we haven't been introduced yet. I am James."

"Finally, a name for the pretty face," I thought.

"Hi, James. I am Sophie. It's nice to meet you," I replied while focusing hard to keep a straight face.

I had always struggled to hide my emotions, and as I didn't want to reveal my feelings for James, I turned myself towards Mo. Maybe this had offended James, for he stepped away from us. He was still within earshot but not really part of the little assembly anymore. He lit a cigarette and looked in my direction. It was obvious that Mo enjoyed my attention, but I thought any man should know that a woman will always try to ignore the man she likes.

"Where did you study, Sophie?" Mo asked.

"I studied in Ireland. Wexford, to be precise. It really was an awesome time. I could walk every day on the beach, and the people in Ireland were so friendly and so much fun."

"Ireland is amazing," Mo said.

"Have you ever been?" I asked.

"No," he replied.

"So, how would you know?" I asked him.

James snorted, which I found very funny.

"I saw pictures and heard people talk about it," Mo answered.

"Sure, this makes sense," I replied. "Shall we go back upstairs?"

Everybody nodded as we all finished our cigarettes. I very much regretted that I hadn't spoken to James more, but at least I knew his name now. Just as I sat down at my desk, I received a call from my manager, Iris. She reminded me of the new starter call on Monday and asked if I would prefer to work from home that day, for the call was at seven in the evening.

"I would love to work from home on Monday," I replied.

"Great, I will inform Dylan. Have a lovely weekend,

Sophie."

I wished her a lovely weekend and hung up. Straight after the call, I went to Vince to inquire if he had a laptop bag for me. Thank goodness he got one. I was just packing my equipment when Mo came walking towards my desk.

"Hi, Sophie. Why are you taking your laptop with you?" he asked.

"I have a new starter call late on Monday, and my manager told me I should work from home that day."

"Working from home is the best. You are going to love it. Do you have a charger?"

"Yes, I do have a charger. Otherwise, my laptop would have died a long time ago," I replied, thinking that Mo was a bit dumb.

"Yeah, but it's better to have a spare one if you forget it at home when you return to the office on Tuesday. I will get you one."

"Sure, why not?" I replied.

Mo went off and returned a couple of minutes later with a charger in his hand.

"Thanks," I said.

He apparently wanted something from me, but his efforts didn't appeal to me at all. I asked myself if my tone of voice had revealed that.

"You are welcome, Sophie. You enjoy working from

home on Monday."

"Thanks. Have a nice weekend," I replied.

"Thanks, see you Monday."

"You mean Tuesday?"

"Yes, Tuesday," Mo answered.

His tone of voice had been aggressive. It was obvious that he hadn't liked it that I had pointed out his mistake, but then he smiled. I thought I had just imagined a change in his behaviour.

Working from home on Monday was indeed very pleasant. I particularly enjoyed the quiet. An additional benefit was the extra hour of sleep, of course. On Tuesday, at about ten in the morning, I approached Mo. He was sitting not far from James, which made me nervous.

"Hi, Mo, here is the charger. Thanks again," I said.

"You are welcome, Sophie. Have you ever visited the United Arab Emirates?"

I asked myself where he was going with this.

"No, I haven't. But I always wanted to see a horse race in Dubai. I'm mad about horse racing; they have some of the best horses there."

I noticed that James was watching us and wondered if it meant anything.

"That can easily be arranged," Mo replied.

"You want to take me to a horse race in Dubai?"

"Sure, it's easy."

"Sure," I retorted sarcastically, but Mo noticed nothing.

"I am glad you like it.".

I wasn't able to understand why he hadn't heard my undertone.

"I have to go back to my desk now. Thanks again for the charger."

"Anytime, Sophie."

CHAPTER 3

Two weeks later, we had a companywide stay in a hotel. On the morning of the meeting, I met Brigitta in the elevator.

"Hi," I said.

"Hi," she replied in a disrespectful tone of voice.

I noticed her resemblance to an angry pug again.

"Do you know how to get to the hotel where the meeting will occur?" I asked her.

"Why would you do that?" she asked.

I was shocked. The answer was not just rude but also brainless, for it had no connection to the question.

"I meant if you could please give me the directions to the location of the hotel, where the companywide will take place," I replied, hoping that this time she would be able to comprehend what I was saying.

"I don't know," she replied.

Something was wrong with her. I instantly regretted that I had even talked to her. As soon as I entered the office, I noticed James. He looked very handsome. He wore a blue blazer, blue jeans, and brown leather shoes.

"You dressed up?" a co-worker asked him.

James straightened himself up.

"Yes, then she will be really impressed," he replied.

"Yes, she looks really impressed," the co-worker said in a sarcastic tone.

I had no idea which girl James wanted to impress, but I found the co-worker's comment somewhat amusing. As Brigitta couldn't give me directions, I asked another co-worker. He pointed out to me that the hotel was just across the street from the office. At about three in the afternoon, I went there by myself. The hotel was fancy, making me feel insecure, for I was very casually dressed that day. I asked at the reception for directions to the meeting room.

"It's on the third floor," the front desk agent responded.

Most employees from CooperateEvent were already present when I entered the room. I chose an empty seat close to the entrance. As soon as I sat down, a ginger-haired guy addressed me.

"Hi, what is your name?" he asked.

"Sophie, what is your name?"

"John."

He appeared to be very friendly. He wasn't my type, but the way he spoke made me think he was very intelligent.

"Nice to meet you," I replied.

"What's your position in the company?" John asked.

"My job basically is to create event landing pages for a German bank," I replied.

"Oh, amazing. We work in the technology team, too," he replied, pointing at the two people beside him.

"Hi," they said.

"Nice to meet you. What are your names?" I asked.

"I am Daniel, and that's Fiona," he replied.

"Pleasure," I replied.

Dylan, who had been sitting in the front, stood up and announced that the meeting was about to start. The conference was indeed very boring. After ten minutes, almost everyone took their phone out, and hardly anyone paid attention anymore. One hour later, we had a fifteen-minute break. My addiction drove me to rush downstairs to smoke a cigarette. Back upstairs, I saw James alone in the meeting room with a beer in his hand. When he saw me, he straightened himself up. "Why is he in here by himself?" I was asking myself.

Although I liked James, I felt awkward being alone in the room with him. I went back outside, where everyone was assembled. The snacks the company had provided looked delicious, and as I had not yet had supper, I helped myself to some king prawns and a glass of wine. James came outside shortly after John had engaged me in a conversation. When he saw that I was occupied, he went back inside the meeting room. "Does that mean that he likes me?" I thought.

After the meeting, Dylan announced that we would all go to the pub and that the drinks would be paid for by the company. I followed my co-workers to the location in silence. The first thing I noticed when I entered the pub was that James was sitting by himself at the end of the bar. I was asking myself why a guy that good-looking wasn't more social. There was a group of Indian-looking people, which consisted of two guys and one girl. They all looked very friendly and approachable. Therefore, I went over to them and introduced myself.

"Hi, my name is Sophie. Do you work for CooperateEvent as well?"

"Hi, Sophie. Yes. We all work for CooperateEvent. My name is Piri. This is Dinesh, and that's Gausika."

I liked Piri immediately. I liked all of them. There was something very open and amiable in their manners.

"Where are you from?" I asked.

"We are all from Sri Lanka," Piri replied.

"Oh, amazing. My housemate is from Sri Lanka. I have

never been there, but I would very much like to go one day," I said.

"Your housemate is from Sri Lanka? Where are the odds in that?" Piri said.

He was clearly the most chatty one. He smiled. It was a very genuine and kind smile. I knew enough about humans to know, without a doubt, that this was a good person.

"Yeah, it's a coincidence. It's great because I like Sri Lankan people a lot."

They clearly liked that. Gausika seemed a bit shy but had a sweet smile and a pleasant disposition. After an hour, I went out for a cigarette, where I met some other employees from CooperateEvent. As soon as I lit a cigarette, James came out, too. They were talking about the company meeting.

"It was a complete waste of time," one employee said.

"I think it was a shame that they were just talking about numbers. I think the meeting could have been way more interesting when they would have talked more about people," I contributed to the conversation.

"Well, business is all about numbers," James said.

"True, but in the end, business is made by people, and people want to be excited about something. When you manage to bring a certain passion across, then you increase sales in the long run," I replied.

James looked rather impressed, which made him even

more handsome in my eyes.

"True, very true," he replied.

Most people were leaving when we entered the pub again. I said my farewells and went home. I was pleased that I had managed to have a conversation with James but wondered which girl he had dressed up for. Was there a possibility that it could have been me?

The weekend was again very dull and lonesome. I told Asiri that I had a crush on a co-worker. He recommended that I wait and let time reveal if there was a chance for romance. He told me that he once had a crush on a girl but that he had always been too shy to talk to her. I very much hoped that this would not be the case with James and that the ice had been broken between us. On Monday morning, we all received an email that informed us that we should have moved to the new office in two weeks, but the engineering work in the building, which was located close to Paddington station, didn't go as planned and we all would have to work from home for one week. The office relocation was displeasing, as the commute time would increase in length. Working from home, however, was always welcome. On the following Friday, I met James in the elevator.

"Hi, how is it going?" he asked.

I had headphones in my ears and took them out while he spoke.

"I meant, how are you?" he added.

"I am good, super happy it is Friday," I replied.

"Yep, almost weekend. Who is not happy about the weekend?" he said.

I didn't dare smile at him because I didn't want to reveal my feelings for him. A rejection would not have been the end of the world, but it could have been embarrassing if it had come from someone I was working with. The possibility was there, however, that James got the impression that I didn't enjoy talking to him that much because my behaviour towards him was very reserved. I assumed that he liked me, but although I was infatuated with him, I wasn't sure if I would have really enjoyed being in a relationship with such a guy, for I was kind of intimidated by his good looks.

The week working from home was pleasant. I could sleep one hour longer every morning, which benefited my well-being, and the lack of distractions increased my productivity. The best part of it was that it snowed on Saturday before I returned to the new office. I looked outside of my window at eight in the evening and felt the excitement pulse through my veins, for it was snowing pretty heavily. I always considered the first snow of the year to be something magical. I couldn't keep the joy to myself. I knocked on Asiri's door.

"It snows," I said.

"I know, it's so beautiful," he replied.

"Do you want to join me for a cigarette outside?" I asked.

"Sure, can I have one?"

"No problem."

In front of the house, we lit our cigarettes and watched the snow fall down from the sky, sticking to the ground.

"How is it going with your crush?" he asked.

I told him that we had talked in the elevator and that I thought he liked me, but I also confessed that it didn't seem to go anywhere so far.

"Just wait. Let him come to you. He must show you he is interested because he is the man."

I knew that he was right, of course. There was nothing less appealing to a man than a girl who was running after him.

Chapter 4

Snow was still on the ground the day I had to return to the office, but it was wet and displeasing. The cold weather made it very inconvenient to find the place. When I entered the building, I saw Ugne, the business support manager, handing out the access badges. There was a queue but the waiting time was of short duration.

"Hi, Sophie. Here is your access card. You will be sitting beside Vince at the desk just on the right next to the entrance," she said.

I took the card and thanked her.

"Our office is on the third floor. When you exit the elevator, turn left."

"Will do. Cheers."

Once I entered the office, I caught sight of Vince.

"Hi, Sophie. You are sitting just next to me," he said.

"Hi, Vince. Ugne told me. It's great," I said and smiled at him.

Gausika approached our desk at the moment that I had begun to take the equipment out of the laptop bag.

"Hi, Sophie," she said with a huge smile.

"Hi, Gausika. Will you be sitting at our desk?" I asked.

"Yes, I think they want everyone from the same department sitting at the same table," she replied.

"Makes sense," I answered.

One hour later, I rolled a cigarette.

"Oh, you're going out for a smoke?" Gausika asked.

"Yeah, I need one."

"I am coming too. Can you give me a minute? I will roll one as well."

"Sure, no problem."

Gausika was very small and had long, dark and curly hair. She had bad acne and missed some teeth, but was still very pretty. However, I could tell she probably felt a bit insecure about her appearance. In my opinion, this made her more amiable, for girls who were too self-assured always had made me feel a bit uncomfortable. It turned out that Gausika had studied design as well. We both agreed that we had managed to acquire decently paid jobs, but we both were disappointed that we hadn't managed to find employment which provided creative opportunities.

Gausika and I took from then on regular smoking breaks together. As Gausika was required to attend a meeting on Tuesday morning, I went out for a smoke by myself. The only employee from CooperateEvent standing outside the building was Mo. "Oh god. Not him," I thought.

"Hi, Sophie. How do you like the new office?"

"It's ok. I preferred the Oxford Circus office."

"Yeah, it's not that nice. You should see the offices close to the back exit of the Paddington station. You can see over Little Venice from there."

"Little Venice?"

"You have never been to Little Venice?" he asked.

"No," I replied.

"Ah, you have to see it. It's very nice," he said with a grin on his face.

"OK, sounds worth a visit."

I had finished my cigarette, and so had he. Therefore, we decided to go back upstairs. He held the door open for me, which could be considered a fine gesture. From that moment on, Mo came out for a cigarette every time I went out by myself.

"Do you follow me?" I asked the third time.

"A little. You should get a restraining order."

I laughed. The comment certainly had been amusing. I didn't consider the possibility that there was truth in his statement. It was obvious that he enjoyed that he had succeeded in entertaining me, for there was a huge smirk on his face, which didn't benefit his looks.

"How old are you?" he asked.

"I am thirty years old. And you?"

"I am twenty-nine."

"Do you live by yourself?" he asked.

"No, I share a place in Finsbury Park."

"You lied to me. You said you live close to Tottenham," he replied.

"I don't even know where Tottenham is. So how could I tell you that?"

"Ahhh... I am pretty sure you said that. Never mind."

"Where do you live?" I asked.

"I rent a studio in Hampstead. I absolutely love it. You should totally come and visit sometime."

"Sure, why not."

I hardly had any friends in London, and the weekends were often dull and lonely. Therefore, I considered the possibility of spending time with him despite the fact that I didn't consider him to be trustworthy. The next day, Mo came out when I was smoking with Gausika.

"Oh, hi, Sophie," he said to me.

"Hi," I replied.

"My name is Mo," he said to Gausika.

"My name is Gausika or Gausi."

"Are the two of you friends?" he asked.

"Well, we don't know each-other that long. We regularly go out for cigarettes together," I replied.

"Oh, great. This company is a great place to make friends," he replied. "Are you religious?" he asked Gausika.

"We identify as Buddhists in Sri Lanka, but I don't really follow the Buddhist teachings," she answered. "And you?" Gausika asked.

"I am Muslim," he replied.

I looked away. I wasn't a racist, but there were many things I disagreed with when it came to Islam.

"I don't care what anyone believes in as long as they don't bother me with it," Gausika said.

"I just want to believe in faith," Mo replied.

Again, I got the impression that Mo just said what he thought others would like to hear. He certainly wasn't following the teachings of the Quran, as he was smoking and drinking. Gausika, however, appeared to like him. She smiled on the way up to the office.

On Thursday, Mo asked me if I wanted to join him for a cigarette. I had no objections, as Gausika was in a meeting. Outside, we joined a group of other employees of CooperateEvent. Among them was James.

"Do you have any plans for Saturday?" Mo asked.

“No, I haven’t.”

“A mate of mine plays with his band in a pub. They are really good. Would you like to join me?” he asked.

I hesitated for a moment and looked at James, who had been watching me.

“Ahm, yeah. I could do that. Why not?”

James instantly looked upset, for his eyelids were contracted. It was so obvious that he didn’t like it that I had agreed to go out with Mo.

“Great, I will be just sitting there by myself, but you can bring whoever you want,” Mo answered.

“Sure, will do.”

“You can, of course, also come by yourself if you prefer,” he added.

“I will see. When does it start?” I asked.

“I will be there at eight. You can come whenever you want.”

“OK, how do I get there?”

“I will send you the address with Teams.”

He did precisely that five minutes after we had returned to the office.

“Thanks, I am sure it will be really fun,” I answered.

“It will be Inshallah,” he replied with a smiley face at the end.

The word “Inshallah” was foreign to me, and therefore, I

had to search for its meaning on the internet. The translation was "if Allah wills it." It didn't displease me that Mo believed in God or Allah, but I was in doubt if a god did exist. Back home, I felt the need to discuss Mo's invitation with Asiri.

"A guy from the office asked me to go out with him on Saturday."

"The guy you have a crush on?"

"No, this is another one. He is Muslim."

"He is Muslim? He won't marry you. Muslim men like to go out with European women, but they never get serious with them."

"I know. I wonder if I should meet him anyway. It probably would be more fun than spending Saturday at home and watching TV."

"You can go, but it has to be just for fun."

"Yeah, it would be just for entertainment. But I am concerned that when he would try to kiss me, I would have to reject him. I wouldn't know how he would react."

"He could get upset if you refuse him," Asiri replied.

"I will think about it," I answered.

We finished our cigarettes and went back upstairs. Back in my room, I considered my situation. On one side, I was bored and wanted more excitement in my life. Mo was sometimes a real idiot, and his constant accusations that I was lying to him were concerning.

"Maybe he is just joking," I said to myself.

More important, however, was that I had no romantic interest in Mo, and therefore, I regretted agreeing to go out with him, especially in front of James. I didn't want James to think I was the kind of woman who would go out with anyone. On Saturday morning, I sent Mo a text with the office communication app as I didn't have his mobile number.

"Hi, I have a flu. I won't make it today. I am sorry."

He didn't reply, and I had no idea whether he had received and read the message or not. The entire weekend was dull, which resulted in me regretting not going out with Mo. A voice in my head told me that I had made the right decision not to go out with him, but I wanted to live a life more invigorating than my current one. My job lacked excitement, and my social life was none existent. Additionally, I had a bit of a bad conscience because I had stood Mo up.

On Monday morning, I went out with Gausika for a smoke. When we came back, we encountered Mo and his friend Amange at the entrance. I greeted him, but he didn't reply. They both walked just past us, looking angry. A part of me was thinking, "Yes, I am rid of Mo. He won't bother me ever again." But then I felt bad. When they came back from their cigarette break, I heard Mo say, 'I said if I ever would marry one, it would be her. But apparently, this is not going to happen.' It made me feel guilty. My bad conscience made me go after Mo when I saw he went out for a cigarette alone one hour later. He was talking to another co-worker when I stepped out of the office building.

"Hi," I said.

"Hi," Mo replied.

He looked uncomfortable and a bit shy. Somehow, this made him more pleasant. The other co-worker had just finished his cigarette.

"I am sorry about Saturday. But I was not feeling well, therefore I couldn't come. I texted you on Teams as I didn't have your number."

"Don't worry about it."

The other co-worker left, and Mo and I were outside alone. He took out another cigarette.

"Do you want one?" he asked.

"Sure, why not?" I replied.

He gave me a cigarette.

"Thanks. Did you have a good time anyway?" I asked.

"Yes, I was there by myself, but the band was really good."

"Great, it's unfortunate that I missed it. Sounds like it was a lot of fun."

Mo seemed to take that as an encouragement because he suddenly appeared to be a lot more cheerful. A voice inside my head told me that I had just made a huge mistake and that I should have been happy when he would have left me alone.

The problem was that nobody in the company was as chatty as Mo. Gausika was a very nice girl, but she wasn't really exciting. Although I didn't trust Mo, something was interesting about him. I was overthinking the whole time, and Mo didn't seem to think at all before he opened his mouth. A few days later, I saw Mo and his friend Amange smoking outside. I went over to join them.

"Hi, Sophie. Do you know Amange?"

"We haven't been introduced yet."

"Hi," Amange said.

"Hi," I replied.

"You look very slim. How do you stay like this? Do you have a strict diet?" Amange asked.

"Me? No. I mostly eat burgers. Sometimes I even eat burgers for breakfast," I replied. This was true. I didn't need to watch my weight.

"That is my girl. Eating burgers for breakfast," Mo said.

"Ach," Amange added.

Mo's presumption had annoyed me.

"I thought you were gay," I said to Mo.

"Seriously? I think I got a reputation with the girls. Everyone knows that," he said.

"Good to know," I thought. I knew that Mo wasn't gay,

but I also didn't want to let him get away with his imprudent remark.

"Do you want to take the stairs?" Mo asked once we had entered the building.

"Sure, why not?"

"Come on. I will race you."

We both started running.

"I won," I said when we reached the top.

"You were on the inside. That doesn't count."

"Yes, it does," I answered.

I enjoyed the race. Although Mo sometimes said stupid things, he managed to make my days in the office a bit more interesting and livelier.

CHAPTER 5

A week prior to Easter, I was smoking outside with Gausika and Mo.

"What do you guys have for lunch?" Mo asked.

"I probably just grab a sandwich somewhere," I replied. "Any you?" I asked.

"Same, or get some Chinese. What do you have, Gausika?"

"I cooked something and brought it with me. It is not that good, though. I prefer my mother's cuisine. She is a great cook."

"Oh, really? You could get her to cook for all of us and bring it to the office?" Mo said.

I thought that was a rather bold move.

"Sure, I can ask my mother to do that. I can bring it just before Easter."

"Great, I am looking forward to it," Mo said.

I kept quiet, for I had the suspicion that Gausika had a bit of a crush on Mo. She never said anything about it but always seemed to lighten up when Mo was around. If Mo had asked me to cook for him, I would have replied, 'Do I look like your mother.' Mo was really impudent. He once told me that I should take the cigarette bud and put it in the bin for him because women in his country were supposed to do what men tell them to do. My response to this insolence had been, 'But you're not in your country, so you might as well adjust.' My retaliation had made him deeply uncomfortable. He even had said so himself. I asked myself if he knew that a behaviour like this was highly inappropriate.

The day before the Easter weekend, I walked into the office and noticed they had been busy decorating the place. There were chocolate eggs on the tables and Easter decorations on each wall. It was kind of cute. Just when I sat on my chair, I heard Mo say to his friend Amange, 'What I am going to do now is stop showing Sophie that I care.' I was wondering what kind of game he was playing. At about ten o'clock, Gausika and I went out for a cigarette and met James. He was standing there by himself.

"Hi," he said to me with a smile on his face.

"Hi," I replied.

I became nervous. When James went back inside, I told

Gausika that I had a crush on him.

"He is really handsome, but I think he likes to drink a lot."

"Really? What makes you say that?" I replied.

"Every time we saw him outside the office, he had a beer."

I thought that hardly said anything, as people often had a drink at social gatherings. At twelve, Gausika informed everyone that the food her mother had cooked was in the kitchen.

"Thanks, but I am not that hungry," I answered.

"Oh, suit yourself. It probably would be a bit too spicy for you anyway," she replied.

Mo came towards our table and sat next to Gausika.

"How is it?" she asked him while making eyes at him.

"It is really good," he replied.

"I am glad you like it," she said with a smile.

At that moment, I saw James walking past our desk. He looked back at me and seemed to have a concerned look on his face. I wondered if James thought something was going on between Mo and me. After all, he had been present the day Mo had asked me out. I felt very embarrassed at that moment. Mo was sitting next to Gausika and not next to me. Therefore, I was concerned that James could have thought Mo had dumped me for Gausika. The thought alone was very humiliating.

"So, do you have any plans for the weekend?" she asked

Mo.

"Oh, yeah. Lots."

He had finished his meal and walked away. He didn't ask Gausika if she had any plans. In my eyes, it was obvious that Gausika had a crush on Mo. Gausika, however, didn't seem to be aware that her feelings and interest in Mo were not reciprocated. I asked her if she wanted to join me for a cigarette.

"Sure, I just need to wait for Mo."

She went over to him and asked if he wanted to accompany us. He answered that it would be his pleasure.

"Are you ok, Sophie? You look really down," he said to me.

I knew why he had asked me that question. He wanted to inquire if it had an effect on me that he had been giving Gausika his attention instead of me.

"I am fine," I replied.

"Oh, good. I would hate to see you sad."

Although I didn't have a romantic interest in Mo, I felt the urge to satisfy my ego at that moment.

"When we were smoking outside in the morning, did you get the impression that he was a bit nervous?" I asked Gausika loud and clear in order to make Mo aware that I was interested in another guy.

"I don't know. I thought I sensed a bit of tension between

the two of you."

"Yeah, but do you think he likes me?" I asked eagerly.

"Could be. I really don't know."

"Why is he never really talking to me then?" I asked.

"He is the kind of person you need to talk to first. He won't come to you," Gausika said.

"Hmm, I don't want to run after him."

Mo had been listening to the conversation. His upset look revealed that. He threw his cigarette on the ground aggressively in response to my revelation.

"I haven't laid eyes on anyone yet," Gausika said when she had seen Mo's angry reaction.

Mo left us and went back upstairs alone.

"See ya," Gausika shouted after him while he was still within earshot.

I was really glad when the day was over. On the journey home, my mind was occupied with the concern that James could have thought that Mo had ended a non-existing relationship. I was well aware that it was a bit silly, but romantic feelings can cloud judgment. I really liked James, but he never engaged me in a conversation, and I didn't want to be the girl running after a man.

Back home, I checked my online bank account. It was a nightmare. The salary hadn't been paid, and I had only five pounds left in my account. The following day was a bank holiday, which meant that the money wouldn't be paid then either. Panic arose inside of me. In order to calm my nerves, I went outside for a cigarette. I was shivering with cold and fear. "Looks like I have no other option but to ask my father for help," I thought. Back in my room, I took my iPhone and called him. He picked up and said nothing.

"Hi, Dad. I have a really big problem and need your help."

"Sophie, you should ask if it is a good time to talk. I told you this many times before."

I felt nauseous.

"But this is urgent. I didn't get paid. I don't know why. The salary should have been in my bank account today, and I only have five pounds left. Can you please transfer me a hundred pounds with Western Union?"

"Why do you only have five pounds left? You should always have a hundred pounds on the site for such a case."

"How should I have saved any money? I got only paid half the salary last month as I started to work in the middle of the month and I had to pay the rent and spend money on food, transportation and utility bills. Can you please send me some money now or not?"

"I won't do it straight away. I am busy. I can do it on Saturday morning."

"Why can't you do it today?"

"You can't always expect people to jump just because you

don't have your life under control."

I got really upset, but in my fear that he wouldn't send me any money at all, I kept quiet.

"OK, then please do it Saturday morning. I don't even have any money for food," I replied.

"Take it as a lesson. I am sure it will teach you to live more sparingly in the future."

"OK, please let me know once you have sent it."

"Will do. Goodbye."

The conversation with my father had made me feel worse. I wanted to turn on my heater as it was cold in my room. Just as I switched the power button, I heard a click. The heater was broken. "This is just great," I said out loud.

On Saturday at eleven in the morning, I called my father again.

"Hi, did you already have a chance to send the money?"

"Don't stress me. I am on my way now."

"OK, thanks. Please send me a message once it is done."

"Will do."

He hung up. At twelve, I got a text from him. He had transferred the money. I went to the closest Western Union store and showed the cashier my passport, but my father had forgotten to include my second first name. Therefore, they didn't allow me to collect the money. I called and told him about his mistake, but he refused to send it again. The entire weekend, I had only a bit of pasta. I was freezing, and I was hungry. In order to distract myself, I created a Tinder account and corresponded with my matches. On Easter Monday, I informed Asiri about the situation and asked if he could lend me some money. He reproached me for not telling him sooner and loaned me fifty pounds without hesitation. A major problem, however, was that I couldn't pay the rent on time. The money was still not in my bank account on Tuesday morning, so I had no choice but to call Iris. She expressed her shock and promised to immediately inquire about what had happened. I had to work from home that day as I had no money to commute. At eleven, Iris called me. The salary hadn't been paid because they had forgotten to add Faster Payment to my transaction. One of the company managers offered to lend me the money under the condition that it would be deducted from my next salary. At twelve, I informed Iris that my Wi-Fi didn't work anymore. Therefore, I had the rest of the day off. "This was one shitty weekend."

Chapter 6

My annoyance hadn't evaporated by Wednesday, for it had truly been a horrendous weekend. With a grim face, I worked resentfully, for I couldn't feel motivated that morning. At ten o'clock, Mo came over to my desk.

"Do you want to come for a cigarette, Sophie?" he asked.

"Yes, just give me a minute, as I have to roll one."

"You can have one of mine."

"Thanks," I replied. "Are you coming too, Gausika?" I asked her.

"No, you two go alone," she replied with disappointment written on her face.

Obviously, she didn't like that Mo had asked me and not her, but I didn't care at that moment.

"Let's take the stairs again," Mo said.

In response, I just nodded. Outside, we both lighted our cigarettes.

"Are you ok, Sophie? You look down lately. Did I do anything that made you sad?"

"It's not you. I didn't get paid before Easter. I had the whole weekend with no money, and I couldn't go out. The heating in the house went out as well, so I was freezing and starving."

Mo had a shocked look on his face, which made him look stupid. "You didn't get paid? What happened?"

"They forgot to add faster payment to my transaction."

"Did you have anyone to help in such a situation?"

"My father tried to send me some money with Western Union but forgot to add my second first name. Therefore, they didn't allow me to collect the money in the shop," I answered.

"Brilliant, they will have to make that up to you. They made you look like a fool. Imaging the consequences when you can't pay your rent on time. Your landlord could have kicked you out."

"I spoke with my landlady and explained, but it was uncomfortable. Margaret told me that my team, which works in Germany, once didn't get paid for two months."

"Don't believe anything Margaret tells you. She once sent my pay slip to the address of another employee. Imagine that."

"Well, Iris, my manager, confirmed that story. It happened."

"Well, they will have to give you compensation for that. Let me make it up to you right now. Let's go for a drink."

"What? Right now?" I asked.

"Now, let's run there."

I smiled, for I felt rebellious at that moment. Mo started running, and I followed him. The pub Mo chose was not too far from the office, but well concealed from the eyes of walking by pedestrians. I doubted that anyone from the office would spot us going in there. Inside, Mo was eyeing himself in the huge mirror that covered the entire wall behind the bar while adjusting his hair.

"Are you checking your curls? You know I am not that much into vanity," I said.

"I just want to make sure everything still sits," he replied while the bartender walked towards us.

"What are you two having?" he asked.

"Two gin and tonics, please," Mo replied, taking his bank card from his pocket.

"Let's go outside. There is a place at the back of the bar where we will be well hidden. We can smoke there," he said.

"Can I tell you something?" I said once I had lighted my cigarette.

"Sure," he replied.

"I hate this job. I came to London to be a graphic designer. Now all I do is copy and paste."

"You just got to keep applying, and maybe you also need to consider applying in other cities, such as Amsterdam."

"I know, but it is really hard. They all ask for experience. How should I get experience if nobody is giving me a chance? I mean, what should I do? Sleep with a creative director."

I said it as a joke but didn't know if Mo understood it.

"Do you keep working on your portfolio? You might need to do some private projects," he said.

"Yes, I do sometimes at the weekend. It just sucks. I thought I would graduate and then get a cool job, which I would enjoy."

"Well, at least you got a good-paid job now."

"They pay me well, but it is not just about the money. I want to live a life of passion, excitement and love. I don't mean just the love for a man. I mean the love for what I am doing," I replied. "What is your dream?" I asked.

"Me? I am interested in the latest technologies," he replied.

"Can I now tell you something, Sophie?" he asked.

"Sure, go ahead."

"I think you are perfect. From the moment you stepped into the office, I had my eyes on you."

"What exactly do you want from me?" I asked.

"I just really like you."

He stepped forward and tried to kiss me, but I stepped back.

"You know. I like you. But this is never going to happen. You're Muslim," I said.

Both my parents had told me that I should never enter into a relationship with a Muslim man, for their religion required them to marry a Muslim woman. Asiri had told me the same when I informed him that Mo had asked me out on a date.

"Oh, come on now, Sophie. You can't just put me in the same box as the rest of them."

"My housemate told me that fifty-year-old men marry ten-year-old girls in the United Arab Emirates and that they have sex with them. This is abuse."

"Some people just interpret the religion the way they want."

"It is wrong," I replied. "How can you stand with them?"

"OK, Sophie. We can talk about this," he said, clearly upset.

"We have been gone for a while. We should go back," Mo said.

I nodded.

"I can't believe this just happened," I said on the way

back.

"Just don't overthink it."

"What? That you just tried to kiss me? You know I don't go out with co-workers."

"Neither do I. This is the first time."

"Yeah, right," I countered.

I doubted that Mo had never gone out with a female co-worker before. We walked in silence the rest of the way. Back in the office, I checked my messages and emails. I had been concerned that someone from my team had noticed that I had been gone for about one hour. Nobody had. It was such a relief. At two, Gausika and I went out for a cigarette.

"Shall we go for a little walk?" I asked.

"Sure," she replied.

"Mo tried to kiss me this morning," I said.

"Yeah? What did you do? Did you go for it?" she asked.

I saw it on her face that she didn't like the news at all.

"No, I said I like him, but it never would happen because he is Muslim."

She giggled.

"I don't think I would have given this reason. Don't worry. He is probably used to it and gets that reason probably a lot."

"I am not a racist. I am just really careful when it comes to Muslim men. They have a different mentality, especially regarding women."

"I am careful too when someone tells me that they are Muslim," Gausika replied.

I was really glad when the day was over. When I left the office, I saw Mo standing outside the office building talking to Amange, but I left without saying goodbye to him. Back at home, I started thinking about Mo and what had happened. I thought that our little excursion had been a bit of an adventure. I hardly ever had fun, for I didn't know many people in London, and Mo had made my day a little bit more exciting. While I considered the day's events, I got a text from a Tinder match. He asked me if I would like to go out with him on Saturday. I hesitated for a brief moment, but then I agreed.

I assumed that Mo had taken the rejection personally and that he probably would stop talking to me. I was very wrong about this. Mo asked me again the next day if I would join him for a cigarette.

"I waited for you yesterday after work, but Amange was there before you," he said.

"That's alright. You didn't need to wait for me."

"I know. I wanted to."

We were standing very close to each-other. A girl from the office approached us.

"Hi, Mo," she said.

"Hi, Jess," he replied.

She looked at us very curiously. I could see on her face that she wondered if something was happening between Mo and me. Back inside, just when I had sat at my desk, Gausika said out of the blue, "You know a friend of mine is such a hypocrite. She said she wouldn't go out with a guy and then did the opposite." I didn't reply. I knew what she had meant. She didn't like that Mo, and I had been going out again without her. Her affection for Mo made her feel resentful towards me, for Mo was giving me his attention instead of her. Having a female friend was important to me, but I knew it would be difficult to maintain a friendship with Gausika when her jealousy took over.

On Friday at half past eleven, Mo and I went out for a cigarette again.

"It's Friday. Let's go for a drink," Mo said.

"Let's do it."

We started running again and made an attempt to cross the pedestrian crossing at full speed, although the light was red. A car nearly hit us.

"What do you think you're doing? Do you want to get killed?" the driver asked.

"Sorry," Mo said while looking very abashed.

"It's ok," I said to him.

He didn't reply. It was obvious that he felt embarrassed

because a stranger had told him off. The rest of the way we walked. Mo insisted on paying again for our drinks.

"What would you like to do right now?" I asked him while we were smoking outside.

"You know. My thoughts actually went in the same direction."

"Maybe you should do it then," I replied.

He leaned down and put his lips on mine. We kissed passionately. Our hands touched each-others bodies. It became wild. I took his hands and then pushed him towards the wall. We nearly fell over.

"I think we are giving everyone a show," he said.

I didn't reply, for I was busy touching his chest. He stepped away and then came behind me. He touched my neck and then then went down on me. He let go.

"Hmmm, we should go back," he said.

I saw that he had an erection.

"People will see that," I said while looking at it.

"It's fine," he replied in a very aggressive tone.

A guy who had been watching us approached Mo.

"Do you want to buy weed?" he asked.

"Yeah, what's your number?" Mo inquired.

"Give me your phone. I type it in."

Mo handed him his phone.

"I will give you a shout later," Mo said once the dealer had entered his contact details.

"Your lipstick is messed up," Mo said just as we had past the Paddington train station.

I wiped my mouth.

"Better?"

"Yes, but only I would have noticed because I was the one who kissed them."

I didn't reply. It sounded to me like he thought he had just won a trophy.

"You know I have so many problems now," I said just before we reached the office.

I didn't know why I had said it. It just had come into my mind, and I let it out.

"I have so many problems now because I am also thinking about eternity."

I thought I knew what Mo had meant. His religion would not have allowed him to get serious with a woman who thought that certain aspects of Islam were wrong.

Back in the office, I caught myself smiling. I was happy. The kiss had been exciting and very passionate. At five, I saw Mo leaving the office with his backpack over his shoulder. He was looking at me on the way out. My head was spinning, and fear arose inside of me. "I can't believe he just left without saying anything," I thought. After a brief moment of hesitation, I went after him. Outside, I only encountered his friend Amange. The fear and confusion must have shown on my face, for he asked if I was ok.

"I am fine. Thanks. Can I have a cigarette?" I asked.

"No problem," he replied while handing me one.

I lighted it and smoked it very fast to release the stress. Mo showed up a couple of seconds later.

"I forgot my charger," he said to Amange.

For some reason, he looked as distressed as I was.

"I have to say goodbye to you," he said. "Amange and I are going to smoke weed. Do you want to come?" he asked when I hadn't replied.

"Yeah, I am coming."

"We have to go and buy the weed. We are back in fifteen minutes. We will wait for you here."

"OK," I replied.

I went back into the office and grabbed my things. Afterwards, I went into the bathroom to refresh my makeup. I also opened my hair, which had been done the whole day in a bun, to make myself more attractive. Once I was happy with my appearance, I went downstairs and lighted another cigarette. Mo and Amange showed up a couple of minutes later.

"Let's go," Mo said.

A little while later, we approached St Mary's Hospital London.

"We just smoke behind it. It's well hidden," Amange said.

"Makes sense," I replied.

Behind the hospital were two benches. There was cardboard on them, which we pushed down carefully.

"Crazy, that is someone's bed," Mo said.

Amange and I just nodded. Mo opened his backpack.

"Look, he bought you something," Amange said.

Mo took a gin and tonic can out and handed it to me.

"I bought you all kinds of flavours," he said.

"Very thoughtful. Thanks," I replied.

I opened the can and lighted a cigarette while Amange was busy rolling a joint. I was watching him.

"Do you want some?" Amange asked.

"No, I am good, thanks. I prefer drinking. You don't drink. Do you?" I asked Amange.

"No, never. I smoke cigarettes and joints. That's all."

"Is it because of the religion?" I asked.

"First, it was because of the religion. Later, it was because it was not good for me. Alcohol can change people."

"Sophie hates all Muslims," Mo remarked.

"Shut up," I said to him.

He laughed. I had no idea what was funny about it.

"I never said I hate Muslims, and I certainly don't. I don't agree with everything Muslims do. Like, for example, old men marry small girls and have sex with them in the United Arab

Emirates," I said to Amange.

"Some people just interpret the religion the way they want," Amange replied.

Funny. That was exactly what Mo had told me. I said nothing because I thought keeping my thoughts to myself was best.

"Do you believe in god?" Amange asked.

"No, I don't," I replied.

"If someone would give you one million pounds, would you be grateful?" Amange interrogated.

"Of course, I would be grateful," I replied.

"Well, it is the same thing. God gave me my life. So, I will be forever grateful," he replied.

I couldn't hold back.

"Your parents gave you your life."

"Well, God gave them their life."

I knew it was pointless to keep arguing.

"Right," I replied.

"Do you believe in a life after death?" Amange asked me.

"Yes, I do. The day my mother died, I kind of had proof that a life after death exists. She was already dead, but then my sister started crying really bad, and she came back. We had to leave the room so she could go."

Mo looked up. I thought I saw a concerned look on his face.

"All that because your sister couldn't stop crying," Amange replied.

"You are quiet, Mo," I said.

"Actually, my thoughts are completely somewhere else," he replied.

I got a feeling, but didn't dare to think about it at that moment.

"But there is something about you. I don't even know what it is. Maybe it's the way you walk," Mo added.

Amange nodded, but I didn't reply. It had been a very weird thing to say when I considered that a couple of days ago, he had told me that he considered me perfect. "Mo must be in a relationship," I thought. His words very much pointed in that direction.

"What are you doing tomorrow?" I asked Amange.

"I am spending the day with my girlfriend."

"Oh nice," I said.

"What are you doing tomorrow?" he asked me.

"I have a date, but I am not hundred per cent sure yet if I will go."

Mo didn't like that. I saw it on his face.

"Do you have any reasons not to go?" Mo asked.

"Not really," I replied.

"Right, then you should go," Mo said.

"I probably will."

Mo nodded.

"Are you still flying on Monday?" Amange asked him.

It was a good call that Amange had changed the subject.

"Yes, I will fly on Monday. I want to see my little brother," he replied.

I suddenly had butterflies in my stomach. It was weird, for I couldn't understand where that feeling had come from.

"Yeah, go and clear your head," Amange replied.

I took another sip from my gin and tonic can.

"What are you doing tonight, Sophie?" Amange asked.

"I go to a party," I lied.

"Oh, nice. And what are you doing tonight?" Amange asked Mo.

"I probably just go home and watch TV."

"Shall we go?" I asked.

Mo and Amange stood up.

"Yeah, let's go," Mo said.

I was in a bad mood but did my best to hide it. As a matter of fact, nobody spoke a word while we were walking.

"That was nice," Mo said at the entrance to the train station.

"Yeah, it was. Have a nice evening," I replied.

"Have fun at the party," Amange said.

"See you," I replied and walked off.

CHAPTER 7

Sometimes, we get a feeling that something is not right about a person or a situation. It can be something a person says or does, but it can be as well just a gut feeling. I had that gut feeling, and I had the thought that Mo's intentions were not good. His behaviour after the kiss pointed in that direction. First, he had intended to leave without saying goodbye. He only had asked me to join him and Amange because I had gone after him. He hardly had said a word when we had been smoking behind the hospital. His limited participation in the conversations had been because his thoughts had been occupied with something or someone else. Before the kiss, he had told me he considered me perfect, but his actions hadn't reflected those words.

On Saturday morning, I was smoking and drinking in front of my house. I never had consumed alcohol in the morning before. It was cold and windy, and it was raining. The weather reflected my mood. I was a good person. Therefore, I couldn't understand why someone wanted to play such a cruel game with me. After two beers, I picked myself up. I spent the whole day looking for an explanation for Mo's behaviour, for I couldn't or didn't want to believe that Mo wanted to hoodwink me. Although I didn't have romantic feelings for Mo, the possibility that he was in a relationship unsettled me, for being deceived like this would be very humiliating. In order to distract myself, I did some research about Islam. My investigation showed that Muslims believe that God will judge them based on their deeds and that their life after death will lie in Jahannam or Jannah. Marrying a Muslim or Christian woman was, therefore, an obligation for Muslim men, for they believed that only a religious woman would spend the afterlife in Jannah, heaven. I concluded that this was the explanation for Mo's strange behaviour.

Although I wasn't excited about my date, I made the necessary preparations. I took a shower, chose an elegant outfit, got dressed, applied my makeup and styled my hair. I wore black jeans, a white t-shirt, a grey blazer and black leather boots, which I had purchased with my first salary. I was happy with the reflection I saw in the mirror. At six in the evening, I took the underground to Oxford Circus. I had to walk only five minutes until I found the place. The ambience of the bar was nice, but a bit too elegant for my taste.

I was fifteen minutes early. While I was waiting, a Muslim man passed me. Six Muslim women were walking behind him. I concluded that they were Muslim because the women were wearing burkas. He was the typical image of an Arab and thought that the women in his company were probably his six wives. I was aware that my thinking demonstrated a lot of prejudice, but I couldn't help myself, especially after Mo's strange and inappropriate behaviour. My date showed up punctually.

"Hi, Sophie."

He gave me a kiss on the cheek.

"Hi, Tim. It's nice to meet you."

"Shall we go inside?" he asked.

"Sure," I answered.

"Should we first go to the bar and get our drinks?" I asked him.

"They do table service here," he replied.

"Great, so what made you choose this bar?" I asked.

"They have great cocktails, and it looks very posh."

"It looks very nice indeed."

A waitress came to take our orders just after we sat at a round table.

"I have a cosmopolitan," Tim said.

"I have a gin and tonic, please."

"So, what are you doing for a living, Sophie?"

"I work for an event software management company. My job is basically to design event landing pages for a German bank. What are you doing for a living?"

"I am a developer. I do a lot of Html, CSS and PHD."

"Ah, cool. We learned how to code Html, CSS and PHP in college. But I hated PHP. It was an absolute nightmare," I replied.

The waitress came with our drinks.

"This cocktail is so good," he said after he had taken the first sip.

Tim was a cute guy, but he wasn't exactly my type. He had blond hair and blue eyes, was athletic, and was about as tall as me. He was good-looking, but I preferred men with brown or black hair. Tim was clearly a well-educated man. We talked about art, design and politics. After about two hours, we visited a hotel bar and looked at a design book. Tim had suggested it because he had thought I would enjoy it. The hotel was very fancy, and I liked the experience, for I had a strong interest in interior design. After Tim had given me the tour, I told him that I wanted to go for a cigarette.

"It was a very nice evening," I said to him.

"I enjoyed it too," he replied.

He leaned down and kissed me. The kiss was nice but not passionate at all. For me, it lacked excitement.

"I think I will go now," I said with a smile.

"Sure, we don't want to rush it," he said.

I kissed him again and wished him a good night.

I was rather tired on Sunday and spent most of the day in bed. I got a text from Tim at three in the afternoon. He asked if I wanted to play pool with him the following Saturday. I replied that it would be my pleasure. Mo wasn't in the office on Monday, but it didn't surprise me, for he had said he would fly somewhere to meet his little brother. At eleven, I was able to overhear a conversation between Ugne and Dylan as they were standing not far from my desk.

"She looks absolutely devastated. Almost as devastated as I was. I told you he is not a very nice man," she said.

Dylan just made a noise but didn't reply. Ugne had gazed in my direction when she had said it. Mo had apparently lied to me when he told me he had never been with a woman from the company before. I didn't know the entire story, but I knew from then on, that Ugne had been devastated because of Mo. Ugne hadn't said his or my name, but as she had been looking at me, I knew who had been meant. From that moment on, I considered Mo as a lying and deceitful imbecile. At lunch, Gausika and I went out for a cigarette. I told her that Mo and I had kissed last Friday and that I regretted it. I informed her that I started dating another guy.

"I just hope that Mo won't be too sad when he hears that I started seeing someone else," I said to her.

"Don't tell him just yet. He could be upset when he hears about it."

I had no proof that Mo was in a relationship, and therefore, I kept my suspicion to myself. I knew that it certainly wouldn't benefit me to reveal my speculation about Mo's cruel intentions. By the time I arrived home, I had made my decision. I messaged Mo on Teams. I informed him that I didn't wish to continue seeing him because we both believed in different things. I could have waited until he was back, but I wanted to be the one who ended whatever we had.

On Saturday, Tim and I met in Central London in the 1920 bar close to the Farringdon station.

"Hi, Sophie. You look very pretty tonight."

I smiled.

"Thank you. You don't look so bad yourself. Are you any good at pool?"

"I am not that good. And you?"

"I am ok," I said.

The price for one hour was fifteen pounds. Tim insisted on paying for it. We played three times, and Tim won every time. I was in a very bad mood by the end.

"You played better in the last game," he said.

"Oh, shut up. You told me you are not good at pool."

"Well, I am not good. You are just really bad."

I showed him my tongue. He laughed.

"Come on. I'll buy you another drink to ease your pain."

We sat outside so that I could smoke. I noticed another couple because the girl appeared to be angry.

"I will practice. The next time we play, I will beat you," I told Tim.

"You do that," he replied.

"You lost as well?" the angry-looking girl asked me.

"Yes, three times. How did you do?" I asked her.

"I lost four times," she answered.

This made me feel a bit better.

"Yes, well, the guys won't get lucky tonight," I said.

"No, they won't," she replied.

We both laughed. Tim and her boyfriend didn't look that happy after my remark.

"Do you want to get another drink somewhere else?" Tim asked.

"Yeah, let's go," I replied.

We went to a pub close by. We stayed for about one hour and then left. Tim kissed me goodbye, and I took the tube home. I enjoyed the evening, for Tim was decent and trustworthy. Therefore, the opposite of Mo. On Sunday, I slept until eleven. When I woke up, I made myself a cup of coffee and went out for a smoke. My thoughts were occupied with the pleasant memories of the previous evening, and Mo was, therefore, forgotten. At one o'clock, I went into the kitchen, where I met Asiri.

"Hi, how are you doing?" he asked.

"I am good. How are you?"

"I am good. Thanks. I need to tell you something. I will move to Manchester in one month."

"Why?" I asked in a high-pitched voice, for this information was far from being welcome.

"Because I will move together with my wife."

Asiri was married. He worked in London because that was the only place where he had been able to find employment, and his wife worked in Manchester. He even had a little boy who was living with his wife and her mother.

"I am really sad that you will move away, but I am happy that you will be with your wife and your son."

"Thanks, Sophie. We will stay in touch."

"Yes, definitely."

This information made me very low-spirited. Asiri had often cooked for me, and the conversations we used to have had always been pleasant. I was aware that I would miss him very much.

"Do you want to come out for a cigarette?" I asked him.

"Sure, just let me get my coat," he replied.

Outside, I told him about the guy I was dating.

"Good for you. He sounds like a nice guy. I am happy for you. What happened with the Muslim?"

"We kissed once, but I don't like him. In other words, I don't trust him."

"Muslims simply have a different mentality. They don't respect women."

"My sister is married to a Muslim. He is good to her," I replied.

"Not all are the same; there are good ones. I say that they are raised differently, especially in the United Arab Emirates."

"Yeah, I know. I have no interest in him."

By no means did I wish to turn into a racist, nor was I one. Some women, myself included, were cautious about dating a Muslim man, for there were many stories out there of non-Muslim women who dated a Muslim man to find themselves deceived and abused in the end. After all the revelations, I could only assume that Mo had been dishonest, and therefore, my prejudice had been confirmed.

CHAPTER 8

A cloud was hanging over me on Monday, making my mood very gloomy. It had not been easy to make friends in London, and Asiri always had been good company. He was a kind and sweet person. The thought that he would leave London made me feel desolate. At the moment when I had sat down at my desk, I caught sight of Mo.

"Look, he is back," Gausika I said.

I didn't reply. He was standing in front of Ugne's desk with Amange beside him.

"You know. I think Sophie is playing games with me," Mo said to Amange.

Mo was looking hopeful and was smirking. Amange was looking at the ground and didn't reply. "Only Mo can believe I am still interested in him," I thought. A couple of hours later, I went to the toilet. On the way back to my desk, I crossed Mo. He was walking next to Brigitta, and both of them were laughing. Curious was that I hadn't seen Brigitta the previous week either, and therefore, I was able to guess who Mo's girlfriend was.

"Hi," Mo said to me.

He smiled, completely unaware of how much I despised him and his deceitful actions. I ignored him, which swiped the grin on his face. A little while later, Gausika and I went for a walk. When we came back, we saw Mo and Brigitta smoking outside the office building.

"The guy I am seeing is so sweet. He always pays for me, and he wants to get to know me before we get active. You know what I mean with active," I said loud enough to make sure that Mo could hear me.

Gausika looked over to Mo.

"He sounds like a keeper," she replied.

I knew that Mo had heard me, for he looked very upset. He aggressively threw his cigarette on the street and returned to the office. Brigitta turned towards me and kept staring at me for about two minutes.

"This girl over there keeps looking at me," I told Gausika.

"Ah, Brigitta. I heard that most people in the office hate her."

"That doesn't surprise me. I asked her how to get to the

hotel, where the company-wide took place. She answered why would you do that."

"What? Is she stupid?" Gausika answered.

I giggled but thought it was unwise to inform Gausika about my suspicion. Most likely because I wanted to spare myself the humiliation of being the victim of deceit. Later in the day, I walked past Mo. This time, he was alone. I acted as if Mo was air, which agitated him. The troubled look on his face made him very ugly indeed. At three in the afternoon, Mo was in a meeting. I observed him from my desk and was pleased that he looked humiliated. By the end of the meeting, they played the song 'Stitches' by Shawn Mendes. Another co-worker gave Mo a hug. "What a convincing victim Mo plays," I thought. I didn't speak to him the entire week. On Friday at four in the afternoon, I met Mo in the lobby. We looked at each other, or better to say that I looked at him defensively.

"Hi," I said.

"How are you doing?" he asked.

"I am good."

"Yeah? Making changes in your life?"

"Yes, I am. I applied for a couple of graphic design jobs."

"Good."

"I am going out for a cigarette," I said.

"I just had one," he answered.

"No worries. Take care," I replied.

He searched my eyes to inquire if I was being serious.

"You too," he said.

When I came back from my cigarette break, Mo's behaviour had changed one hundred eighty degrees.

"I think I want to destroy Sophie's life," Mo said very loud and clear to one of his friends.

He didn't get a response. Hate arose inside of me. It was outrageous when I considered that he most certainly was in a relationship. I thought that he had serious mental health issues and therefore ignored it, but I decided to keep an eye on the situation. At five, Mo walked towards the exit.

"Are you leaving?" a co-worker asked him.

"Yes, I am not staying on more minute in a room with Sophie."

At the end of the business day, I had an ominous feeling. I was wondering if it had been an empty threat or if he had been serious when he had announced that he wanted to destroy my life. On Saturday morning, I woke up and had a bad cold. I took out my phone and texted Tim.

"Hi, Tim. I am sick. Can we please reschedule our date for next weekend?"

Fifteen minutes later I got a reply from him.

"Oh no. I hope it's not too bad. Sure. We can reschedule for next weekend. Get well soon."

"Thanks. I hope you can enjoy the weekend anyway," I replied.

The cold got worse over the weekend and wasn't gone by Monday. As I was still on probation, I didn't dare to call in sick. Mo was acting normal again. "You see. It just had been an empty threat," I told myself. Gausika and I went out for cigarettes by ourselves from then on. Mo was no longer following us, so we turned our attention towards Vince, who appeared to be a nice guy.

"You look happy, Sophie," Vince said to me.

"I am, apart from my cold."

"You are in love. Aren't you?"

"No," I replied.

"How is it going with the guy you date?" Gausika asked.

"It's going well. I had to reschedule the date we were supposed to have on Saturday for next weekend because of this bloody cold."

"Oh no. Do you have any idea what you will do together the next time?" she asked.

"Don't know yet."

I looked up and saw that Mo was watching me. I wondered if he had heard the conversation.

"Are you seeing anyone, Vince?" I asked him.

"Not really. I am using dating apps, but it never seems to go anywhere," he replied.

"I am sure you will find someone very soon," I said.

Later in the day, I overheard Amange talking to Vince.

"Vince, you have to fix Mo's screen." -

It had not been a question but a command. I found it peculiar that Mo had not asked Vince himself, for he had been standing next to Amange when the order had been given. Tim texted me on Wednesday.

"How are you feeling?" he asked.

"I still have a bit of a cough, but I am feeling much better," I replied.

"I am happy to hear it. Do you want to go on a picnic in Hyde Park on Friday after work?" he asked.

"I would love to," I replied.

The cough wasn't gone by Friday, but I didn't dare cancel again. Tim and I met at six o'clock at the Lancaster Gate underground station. He demonstrated how happy he was to see me by kissing me passionately.

"You look very pretty tonight," he said.

"Thank you. You look very handsome yourself."

"Thanks, I brought a blanket."

"Did you bring, by any chance, some food?"

"No, I wasn't thinking about that," he replied.

I rolled my eyes.

"How are we supposed to have a picnic without any food?"

"Hmm, good point. There is a shop close by. Let's go there," he said.

Our picnic consisted of sandwiches, crisps and sodas. Once we had bought the supplies, we went into the park. Tim laid the picnic blanket on the grass. We sat down and started kissing. When our lips parted, he repeated his admiration for my good looks.

"You're so sweet," I replied.

I was hungry and, therefore, took a break from kissing to eat my sandwich, but it didn't satisfy me. After about one hour, we decided to go for a walk.

"You know it's our third date," I told him.

"It is," he replied.

"You know what that means?" I asked.

He smiled.

"I think I do."

We started kissing again.

"Shall we go to my place?" he asked.

"Yes," I replied.

We took the Piccadilly line from Hyde Park corner and changed at Holborn. At Bethnal Green, we went out. I looked around curiously, for I had never been to this area of London before.

"Shall we get drinks before we go to my place?" he asked.

"That's a great idea," I replied.

In an off license not far from the underground station, I bought a couple of gin and tonic cans, and he bought a couple of beers for himself. I was curious how he lived.

"I think my housemates are not home, but I am not sure. So, it's best when we don't make too much noise," he said when we were standing in front of his door.

"Sure, no problem," I replied.

He unlocked the door. His apartment had a big living room and a modern kitchen. He lived much nicer than I did.

"It's lovely. I like it."

"Thanks, I will show you my room now."

"Actually, I have to go urgently to the toilet."

"Sure, it's just in the hallway on the left."

"Tim," I said when I had done my business.

He came out.

"Are you ok?" he asked.

"Yes, I just didn't know where you were."

"You should have come to my room first."

"Makes sense now."

He smiled. I followed him into his room. We started kissing and slowly proceeded to more intimacy. I was coughing a lot, which complicated the matter. The following morning, I woke up way too early. I was craving a cigarette, but Tim's apartment didn't have a balcony.

"Tim," I said.

"Hmmm," he said sleepy.

"Tim," I repeated.

"Yep," he said.

"I want to go out for a smoke. Can I just go down and come back in?"

"You will need the keys. They are in the living room. Do you want me to come down with you?"

"No, you can sleep."

I put my trousers on, grabbed the keys and went downstairs. The night with Tim had been nice. He was good to me, but I was not in love with him yet. I thought love should be butterflies in the stomach, excitement and passion. Maybe that's why I wasn't in love with him. Tim was nice, but he didn't give me a thrilling sensation. After I had smoked my cigarette, I went back upstairs, where I found Tim in the kitchen.

"Do you want to have breakfast?" he asked.

"Yes, please. It would be great to get some coffee," I replied.

"Sure, I am on it."

"Thanks."

"Wow, you know how to make a coffee," I said, for the coffee he had made me was so delicious.

"It's great. Isn't it?"

"It is. Very sweet."

"Just like you." he replied.

He gave me a kiss on the neck just where he had given me a hickey the night before. He made spinach, smoked salmon and scrambled eggs for breakfast. It was very tasty, but I coughed about every other minute.

"You don't sound too good," he said after we had finished our meal.

"Yes, I think that I maybe should go home and get some rest."

"I think you should."

I went into his room and packed my stuff together. Tim was waiting for me by the door.

"Last night was great," he said.

"It was," I replied.

"You get well. I will text you tomorrow."

"Talk tomorrow."

I went outside and made myself on the way to the tube station. My cough was so bad by the time I got home that I went straight to bed. On Monday I was very sick. Going on a date with such a bad cold probably hadn't been the best idea. I went to the office simply because I was still on probation.

"Nice hickey," Vince said to me.

Gausika was looking up.

"That's not a hickey. It's sun allergy," I replied.

"Some sun," Vince said.

I grinned.

"That made me laugh," Vince remarked.

I laughed at myself and then started coughing. Vince left and went over to Mo.

"She got a hickey," I heard Vince say to Mo.

I was asking myself why Vince had told him that. Mo didn't respond. He stood up and left the office. By twelve, my cough was so bad that I couldn't even smoke anymore. I called Iris and told her I needed to work from home because my cough was worsening every minute. She had no objections.

"You need to get that sorted," Vince told me.

"I know," I said while packing my stuff.

"Well, I will see you guys whenever I am well again," I said to Gausika and Vince.

"Get well soon," they both replied.

I didn't feel one bit better when I was back home. I made an appointment with the doctor for the following day. It turned out that I had Pneumonia and that I couldn't work for two weeks. She gave me antibiotics and told me to get plenty of rest. Iris wasn't happy about the news but realized she had no choice but to accept it. Tim texted me later in the day.

"How are you feeling?" he asked.

"I have Pneumonia," I replied.

"Oh shit. I feel really bad now. I shouldn't have asked you

on the date," he replied.

"It was my responsibility. I should have asked you to reschedule again," I replied.

"Well, there is some truth in that. You get well now. Let me know how you feel in a couple of days," he responded.

"Will do. X," I replied.

I was happy I didn't have to work for two weeks, but it got a bit boring after a while. I couldn't smoke anymore, and my only distraction was watching movies on my laptop.

Chapter 9

The time off benefited me greatly. My skin was glowing the day I returned to the office, and I felt an increase in my energy. Gausika was already sitting at her desk by the time I arrived.

"Welcome back," she said.

"Thanks," I replied.

"You look great," she said.

"That's sweet of you."

"I mean, you look a lot better than the last time I saw you," she added.

I grinned.

"All clear," I replied.

Mo walked past me a couple of minutes later. He looked at me while passing my desk. Maybe it was imagination, but he appeared to be relieved to see me. I went for a cigarette by myself at ten o'clock as Gausika was busy. I met Mo when I was walking down the stairs. He took me in his arms and gave me a kiss on the neck.

"Welcome back," he said.

I didn't reply. I was very much taken by surprise.

"Vince told me you were a little bit sick."

"I am ok now."

"I am so happy you're back," he said.

He appeared to mean it.

"I go out for a cigarette," I replied.

"See you later," he said.

I had never experienced this warm and caring side of Mo before. It certainly improved my opinion of him. His kind welcome had been genuine. I was certain of it. At that moment, I questioned my judgement of him and asked myself if I had been right about him and Brigitta. Shortly after I had come back from my cigarette break, I got a text from Tim.

"Back among the living?" he asked.

"Yep, I am well again," I replied.

I smiled.

"A text from your man?" Vince asked.

"Yep," I replied.

"How is it going between the two of you?" he asked.

"I am not sure yet, but it is going well," I said.

"Nice," Vince replied.

He stood up and went over to Mo. Was he reporting to him? I didn't really listen to Mo and Vince's conversation because I had just received another text from Tim. He asked me if I wanted to go with him to Hampstead Heath on Saturday. I replied that it would be my pleasure.

"I can't do that," I heard Vince say to Mo very loud and clear.

Although I was aware that I didn't know the context of their conversation, I got the feeling that Mo had asked Vince to do something very wrong and that it involved me. I went out for a cigarette, where I encountered Amange.

"Hi," I said.

"Hi, I haven't seen you in a while."

"Yes, I was sick. I had Pneumonia."

"Pneumonia? Did you get paid for the time you were off?" he asked.

"I think so," I replied.

"Pneumonia is quite serious. Did you have to take antibiotics?"

"Yes, for two weeks."

"But you're good now?"

"Yep, all recovered."

"Do you have any plans for the weekend?" he asked.

"Yes, I will go to Hampstead with the guy I am dating," I

replied.

"Nice," he said.

We finished our cigarettes and went back upstairs. When we entered the office, Mo came walking towards us.

"See you," I said to Amange.

"Where have you been?" Mo demanded.

"Just been out for a smoke," Amange replied.

Again, I felt that Mo liked controlling the people around him. I sat at my desk and started catching up with all the work that had piled up while I had been sick.

"We should probably exchange numbers in case we need to contact each other or if we want to hang out," Vince said.

"Sure, why not?" I replied.

"Great, what's your number? Vince asked.

I gave him my number and saved his in the Contact app. Gausika saved my number as well on that occasion.

Later, I saw Mo and Amange in a meeting room together. Amange was watching me. It appeared to vex Mo greatly. After the meeting, I observed that Mo grabbed his things and left without saying a word. On his way out, he gave me a searching look. I received a call just after stepping out of the Finsbury Park underground station.

"Hello, we were informed that you were involved in a car accident," the woman said.

"I don't have a car. Please do not contact me again," I said and hung up the phone.

"These stupid spam calls," I thought. "Weird, though. The woman on the phone sounded just like Brigitta."

Mo wasn't in the office the next day, but I, however, overheard Amange talking to a co-worker.

"But he is in a relationship," Amange said to Jennifer.

"Yes, but this relationship. She is sitting here and pretending that she is ok with all of that," Jennifer replied.

Amange hadn't said Mo's name, but I was certain he had been talking about Mo and Brigitta. "That piece of shit," I thought.

On Friday, I felt excited as I looked forward to meeting Tim the next day. I had never been to Hampstead. When I walked out of the station, I saw immediately how pretty it was. I knew that Mo lived in this area of London but thought the chance we would meet was very slim. After five minutes of waiting, I received a text from Tim. He informed me that he would be late. In order to bypass time, I went to a local shop and got myself an orange juice. Fifteen minutes later, Tim showed up.

"Sorry for being late."

"It's ok."

In my country, we were always punctual. Therefore, I couldn't hide entirely that I was a bit displeased.

"Let me buy you a coffee," he said.

"OK, thanks."

I followed him.

"Do you know where we are going?" I asked.

"Oh yes. My ex and I used to own an apartment here."

"How could you afford this?"

"We both had very good-paid jobs," he replied.

I thought I would love to live in Hampstead as it was truly delightful.

"Maybe we should also get something to eat," I said.

"Good idea. Take whatever you want. I will pay."

I took a cappuccino and a panini, and he took a coffee and a wrap. We walked for about half an hour in the park before we reached a beautiful place with a view over a pond. We sat on the grass in the shadow of a mighty tree and kissed each other. When our lips parted, I looked in the direction of the ponds, where I saw Amange and Mo sitting on the grass. Was this a coincidence? Mo lived in Hampstead, so it was possible.

"Shall we go somewhere else?" I asked Tim.

"Yes, let's go," he said.

I wanted to get away from that place, away from Mo. Later in the evening, Tim and I went back to Central London, where we had dinner in an Italian restaurant. I ordered a gin and tonic and a pizza.

"I have to go to the toilet," I said after we had finished our meal.

"Sure," he replied.

"Excuse me. Where is the toilet?" I asked the waitress who was passing me.

"Just downstairs on the left," she replied.

I walked one step down, and then I slipped and fell. "Ouch," I screamed. Tim had obviously heard me, for he rushed to my assistance immediately.

"Sophie, are you ok?" he asked.

"I fell. It's a bit sore."

"Do you need help?"

"I think I will be ok," I replied, but I had to limp down. When I came back from the toilet, I ordered two more gin and tonics to ease the pain.

"I will order an Uber," Tim said.

"Maybe not the worst idea," I replied.

I could hardly walk anymore. We spent the night together, but I was still in a lot of pain. The next morning, we ate breakfast from Costa on a park bench. Just when I had lighted a cigarette, I saw Mo. He was standing on the other side of the very small park. Was I losing my mind, or was it just someone that looked a lot like Mo? "Why would Mo be in this area?" I thought. It was, after all, a long distance away from Hampstead. I kissed Tim again and then looked back where Mo had been standing. He was gone.

"I am still in a lot of agony. I would like to go home now,"

I told Tim.

"I understand. Last night was fun despite your accident."

"It was indeed."

"I walk with you towards the underground station."

I was deep in thought on the way home. Was I imagining things? Was Mo stalking me? But it couldn't be. I had overheard Amange saying that Mo was in a relationship. "Why on earth would he have followed me, and, more importantly, how could he have followed me?" I was asking myself. I concluded that I wasn't even sure if I had seen Mo. He had been standing on the other side of the park, so it could have been just someone who had resembled him a lot. On Monday, I had to limp to the office.

"What happened to you?" Gausika asked.

"Me and my date were in a restaurant. I fell down the stairs when I wanted to go to the toilet."

"Ouch, does it hurt a lot?"

"No, I walk around like this for fun," I countered.

She laughed.

"Do you want to come for a cigarette?" I asked.

"Sure, grandmother."

"You wait. I will get you back for this."

She chuckled. Mo was not in the office that day and wasn't in on Tuesday, Wednesday and Thursday. Although I didn't miss him one bit, I kind of wondered where he was and what he was doing. On Thursday, I got a text from Tim.

"Hi, Sophie. How is your hip?" he asked.

"Much better. Thanks," I replied.

"Great, do you want to do something on Saturday?" he asked.

"Sure, what do you have in mind?" I asked.

I waited for his reply, but none came. On Friday, I began to ask myself if Tim had lost interest in me. At half past four, Mo showed up in the office.

"Come on now, Sophie," he said while walking past my desk.

I didn't know if anyone else had heard that, but I found that remark very creepy and concerning. In order to relief the stress, I went out for a cigarette. Tim had asked me out on a date and then hadn't replied anymore. Mo had showed up in the office half an hour before the end of the business day and said, 'Come on now, Sophie.' Was this all a coincidence? I doubted it. The question was whether I should have told anyone about the odd events that took place or not. I decided against it because I knew people would say it was just in my head. Something was certainly not right with Mo, but I thought that if I ignored it, he would capitulate and leave me alone. How wrong I had been about my assumption became apparent the following week. Mo had changed his tactic. Every time he walked past my desk, he looked at me and smirked. I was determined not to honour this behaviour with a reaction.

After a brief period, however, I began to have bad dreams. Mo appeared in every single one of them. The weirdest dream involved Mo showing up on a white bicycle everywhere I went. I couldn't keep this to myself, for I woke up every day at half past four in the morning.

"Can we talk after work?" I asked Gausika during a smoking break.

"Sure, but don't you want to tell me now what is happening?" she asked.

"No, I would prefer to have this chat outside office hours," I replied.

"We can go for a quick drink after work," she said.

"Sounds good," I replied.

At half past five, Gausika and I left the office together. We went to a pub close by. We took our drinks outside so that we could smoke.

"So, do you want to tell me now what is going on with you?" she asked.

"It's Mo. He keeps staring at me. I can't sleep anymore. I wake up at half past four every morning because I have bad dreams about him," I said.

"Do you like Mo?" she asked.

"It's not that. I don't want to go out with him, but he

doesn't leave me alone," I said.

"Then you need to talk to him face to face. Say you like him but that it will never happen."

I looked at Gausika and wondered if I should illuminate her about the full extent of the situation. The fact that I had heard Amange say that Mo was in a relationship would certainly have given Gausika a whole new perspective. I wondered if she would believe me, though.

"What if it will make it worse?" I asked her.

"How could an honest conversation make things worse? You need to tell Mo how you feel. I am sure he will understand. You should also tell Vince. I am sure he will be able to give you some valuable advice."

"OK, will do."

Gausika had to meet her mother, and therefore, we said goodbye. My mind was by no means at ease on the way home. If my interpretation was correct, Mo was and had been in a relationship with Brigitta the day he and I kissed. It was very unlikely that Brigitta didn't know about any of this. Especially when I considered that I had heard Brigitta say to Mo, 'Are you going to talk to her now?' shortly after I started working at CooperateEvent. What troubled me was the possibility that Brigitta had ordered Mo to deceive me, but what kind of woman would make such a request from her boyfriend? Back home, I distracted myself by watching the movie 'How to lose a guy in ten days.' The movie was very entertaining, but it also gave me an idea. Certain behaviours in a relationship were considered highly annoying and off-putting. Mo had tried to deceive me, so I thought it wouldn't be the worst idea to give him a taste of his own medicine.

CHAPTER 10

I bided my time until the right opportunity presented itself. Mo's inappropriate behaviour had affected me grievously, and I was therefore determined to put an end to it by using his weapons against him. The following Friday, we had a kind of after-work party in the office. Gausika, Vince, Piri and I helped ourselves to some beers and snacks.

"Can I talk to you outside?" I asked Vince after I had a couple of drinks.

"Sure," he replied.

When we stepped out of the building, I saw Brigitta and Amange, their presence was most advantageous. To make sure that Amange and Brigitta were able to hear every word I was saying, I spoke loud and clear.

"Mo and I once kissed. Afterwards, I rejected him. Now, he keeps staring at me. I like him but don't want to go out with him," I said.

"When you like him, why don't you want to date him?" he asked.

"It's just that he is Muslim and Muslim men simply have different requirements for a partner. I am not racist. It's just that after Mo and I had kissed, he made this weird comment about eternity. It made me think that he would never get serious with an atheist."

"Well, if you don't want to go out with him, then you need to tell him."

"You think talking to him will help? Gausika thinks so," I said.

"Yes, you should have a chat with him outside of the office."

"Will do that. Thanks, Vince."

I was positive that Amange and Brigitta had heard me, for they both had a smirk. On Monday, I went out for a cigarette at about half past nine. Mo and I encountered each-other at the entrance.

"Hi, Sophie," he said.

I walked past him without reciprocating his greeting. The conversation I had held with Vince had the expected result. I was one hundred per cent certain that Amange and Brigitta had told Mo what they had overheard. Why else would Mo suddenly have talked to me again? "God, he is a piece of shit," I thought. I couldn't keep lying to myself. A part of me was worried about Mo's bizarre and creepy behaviour, but another part wanted revenge. I was therefor delighted that I had managed to mortify him somehow. Mo didn't make another attempt to talk to me for the rest of the week. He ceased staring and grinning at me as well. My plan had worked out.

Sleep still eluded me, however. Bad dreams about Mo woke me up every morning at five. The following day, I went out for a smoke and saw James sitting on the stairs by himself. He looked as handsome as ever.

"Hi," I said.

"Hi, how are you?" he asked.

"I am good. And you?"

"I am good. The weather is so nice. I want to go into the beer garden."

"That's a really good idea."

"You studied in Ireland. Didn't you?"

"Yes, in Wexford."

"Nice, what made you study there?"

"A couple of years back, I was on a horse-riding holiday in Sligo. I just fell in love with Ireland. It was so beautiful. We once rode to a little Island, where we laid on the grass. We had the ocean in front of us and the horses beside us," I replied.

"Sweet."

"Have you ever been to Ireland?" I asked.

"Yep, I am half Irish. We have family over there."

"Oh, nice. Where in Ireland does your family live?"

"Donegal."

"Nice, I have never been, but I heard it is beautiful. It's not far from Sligo," I replied.

"Yes, Donegal is beautiful. It can be a bit cold up there, though."

"I heard that too."

We both finished our cigarette.

"I am going back up," I said.

"Actually, I am coming too," James replied.

We took the elevator and smiled at each-other on the way up.

"See you later," he said when we entered the office.

"See you," I replied.

I beamed. Gausika was watching me, but she didn't ask. On Saturday, Asiri was moving out. At two in the afternoon, he came knocking on my door.

"Hi, I am leaving now. I came to say goodbye," he said.

"I am going to miss you."

"I will miss you too."

"Stay in touch," I replied.

"Will do. I will text you soon."

We hugged each-other. I was downhearted after the farewell, for I knew that I would miss him and feel lonely in the house without him. Mo was not in the office the entire next week. It was always a lot easier to concentrate when he was absent, for I never had to worry about what he might do to unsettle me again. On Thursday, on my way to the bathroom, I had a co-worker, who looked Arab as well, pointing at me.

"This is the one Mo gave up everything for," he told his friend.

"Not bad," his friend replied.

"What the hell was that all about," I thought. I was fed up with this story. Even when Mo was not around, I was still involved with him somehow. A plan formed inside my head to solve that predicament once and for all. The following Monday, Mo was back in the office. At half past four in the afternoon, I sent him a message on Teams.

"I heard someone say something about you. I want to talk to you about it. Meet me at the Prince of Wales pub. I will be waiting there until six," I pressed send.

At five, I left the office. In the lobby, I met Sara. She was another Swiss girl who worked for CooperateEvent.

"Hi, how is it going?" she asked.

"All good. How are you?"

"I am good. What are you up to now?"

"I have to speak to Mo."

"Who is Mo?"

"He is tall and has black curls," I replied.

"The one that walks funny?"

"Yep, that's the one."

"Why do you need to talk to him?" she inquired.

I told her the basics of the story and informed her about my insomnia, which was the result of Mo's irritating behaviour. I refrained myself from telling her all the dirty details.

"I told him he should meet me in the Prince of Wales pub by six tonight," I ended.

"I actually wanted to go to my Yoga class, but I could come with you if you would like to have some company."

"That would be great."

"My pleasure. I am really curious if he will show up."

We went into the pub, ordered drinks and took them outside. We talked about work, living in London and about our dating experiences. At half past six, we went back inside and ordered another drink. As soon we had entered, I spotted Brigitta in the company of two co-workers. I speculated inside my head about the reason for her presence in that particular pub.

"I start to think he is not coming," I told Sara at six.

"I was certain that he would show up," she replied.

At precisely that moment, Mo appeared.

"Hi," he said.

"Hi, this is Sara. I don't know if you know her," I replied.

"We haven't been introduced yet. Nice to meet you," he said.

"Likewise, I was just about to leave," she replied.

"I will text you later," I said in Swiss-German.

"Do that. I want to know everything," she also replied in our mother tongue.

"Have a nice evening," she said.

"You too," I replied.

I waited until she was out of sight.

"Do you want a drink?" I asked.

"No, I am good. I don't drink during the week anymore," he replied. "When you said that you wanted to meet me, I didn't think there would be other people from CooperateEvent here," he said.

"What's the problem?" I asked.

"I just don't want people to talk. There is anyway already enough shit happening."

I didn't reply at first, for I felt anger raising inside. Mo apparently had a problem with people knowing about this. I thought that I would keep that in mind.

"So, how have you been?" I asked him.

"OK, I mean, I really hate my job and want to find a new

one, but apart from that, not too bad."

"Yeah, you should try."

"You said you wanted to talk to me about something. That you heard someone say something about me, I would like to know what it was," he said.

I lighted another cigarette before I replied.

"Yes, last week when you were away, I heard a guy from the office say that I was the one you gave up everything for. I considered that very weird, so I wanted to ask you what the meaning of this is."

Mo's facial expression changed. He looked very uncomfortable.

"Who said that?" he asked in an unsteady tone.

"I don't know his name."

"Then show me on Teams," he requested.

"How could I show him to you on Teams when I don't know his name?"

"Yeah, I suppose you can't."

"So, what is the meaning of this?" I asked.

"Don't believe what people say. They always talk shit and tell lies."

"Good, it's just that you and I never really talked about what happened between us."

"No, we never did," he replied.

"It's a bit uncomfortable sometimes," I said.

"Yeah, and there are a lot of awkward moments when we pass each other."

"Yes, well, I just wanted to let you know that you shouldn't take the rejection personally. I really did like you, but there were just things I didn't want to get involved with," I replied.

I looked deep into Mo's eyes because I wanted to see if he had been able to understand the hint. His irises were very dark and unusually big, but apart from that, I didn't notice anything that would have indicated any discomfort.

"Well, thank you very much, but I need to go now," he replied.

"Sure, you don't want to say anything else? This would be your moment to do so."

"No, I am good. Thanks. I will go inside the pub now and say hi to the people from the office."

"OK, see you tomorrow," I replied.

He didn't respond and walked away. "Interesting." He said he had to go and then went into the pub to meet Brigitta," I thought.

In my opinion, Mo was not supposed to escape the consequences of his deceitful actions and cruel intentions too easily. I took out my phone. "I am glad that you try to make changes in your life, but you also should try to fight for what you want," I typed and pressed send. "This will give Mo two options to interpret. Either I am talking about me or his career. If he wants to mess with my head while he is in a relationship with Brigitta, I will give him a taste of his own medicine," I thought. He wasn't in the office on Tuesday but showed up again on Wednesday. I ignored him and acted like he didn't exist. Vince and I had fun talking about music and even danced around a bit. I was in a really good mood the entire morning. At twelve, Mo came over to our desk. Suddenly, he smashed a computer mouse violently on the table. Gausika, Vince and I looked up. Vince and Gausika looked very uncomfortable. I, however, was shocked. I felt my hands shaking and sweating.

"Jesus Christ. Did you see that?" I asked.

Gausika nodded but didn't reply. When I looked up, I saw Mo kicking open the door to the men's toilet. I grabbed my bag and went outside.

Instead of getting myself lunch, I went into the pub where Mo and I had kissed and ordered a gin and tonic. Outside, I lighted a cigarette but had trouble keeping the glass in my hand steady. I felt scared and was well aware that my plan didn't have the desired effect. Mo's aggressive behaviour indicated a serious mental illness. I was convinced that he was crazy. I had done a lot of things in my life which had been brave and even foolish, but it never would have crossed my mind to kick open a door in an office. "Should I leave the company? I can't. I have no other job in sight, and I still own my sister money. If I quit this job now, I won't be able to support myself anymore," I thought. I concluded that I had no other option but to stay until I found a new job. I was no fool. Mo had acted like this to intimidate me. Maybe it was just threatening behaviour, but it was also possible that he was dangerous. I concluded that it probably would be best to ignore him again. It wasn't easy, however to focus on my work that afternoon. The next day, Mo walked past my desk with his friend Amange.

"And all these made-up rumours. I just wanted to fuck her," Mo said to Amange.

I was outraged. About one hour later, I went out for a smoke. I saw Mo in the lobby with another co-worker.

"She wants me to chase her now, but she is just a pretty girl," he told his friend.

I felt upset and wondered if this would only get worse. Later in the afternoon, I told Gausika what I had heard Mo say.

"He is just trying to provoke you because you're the much bigger person. Just ignore him," she said.

"You said I should have a chat with him, but this just made everything worse."

"Yeah, it was good that you had a talk with Mo. He is just upset because he got rejected. Don't worry. He will stop."

CHAPTER 11

Something inside me had changed. For a start, I dressed differently. My outfits had always been very casual. After Mo's display of violence, my outfits were way sexier as it increased my confidence and made me feel somehow stronger. My alcohol consumption increased, and so did the number of cigarettes I smoked per day. I ate less and lost weight, which benefited my appearance. The lack of sleep had an enormous impact on my physical and mental well-being. I felt constantly exhausted, stressed, agitated, and less in control over my emotions. It was a difficult situation which demanded a resolution. The following Friday, I went out for lunch by myself. When I was walking in the direction of Sheldon Square, I saw Mo in the company of Amange and another co-worker walking towards me.

"Sophie is coming," I heard Mo say to Amange, although

there was quite a distance between us.

Mo turned around and walked in the other direction. Amange winked at me when he crossed me. I nodded to demonstrate that I had seen him. When I had reached Sheldon Square, I spotted Mo sitting outside a coffee shop in the company of three girls. He was grinning when he saw me. I ignored him entirely. In Sainsbury's, I bought a wrap and two gin and tonic cans. I wasn't really hungry; therefore, I drank only my alcoholic beverages below the Paddington Central footbridge, for it was unlikely that I would encounter anyone from the office there. I wasn't drunk when I went back into the office, but a little bit tipsy. Mo entered the office shortly after me.

"I think Sophie didn't see me," he said within my earshot.

Apparently, Mo wanted everyone to believe that I liked him. Ugne came to our desk shortly afterwards.

"There will be drinks and snacks in the kitchen later. Just help yourself when you have finished working."

"Thanks, Ugne," Gausika replied.

At five, Gausika and I went into the kitchen to get some beers.

"Are you not hungry?" she asked.

"No, I had enough at lunch," I lied.

We went back to our desk. At that precise moment, Mo showed up in the company of Amange. Neither he nor

Amange were saying anything. They just stood behind us. I knew it was again an act of intimidation.

"Do you come out for a smoke?" I asked Gausika.

"Sure, give me a minute," she replied.

"Are you ok?" she asked when we were outside.

"Yeah, I am fine," I replied.

"Your hands are shaking," she observed.

"I know. I just don't sleep too well lately. I have funny dreams."

"Yeah, what are the dreams about?"

"They are mainly about Mo."

"Something dirty?" she asked.

"Not really. It's always the same dream. Mo shows up wherever I go on a white bicycle."

"That's weird."

"Yeah, it's annoying. I don't feel good when I can't sleep right. I wake up every morning at five, and it really starts to get to me," I said.

"Yeah, I am the same. When I can't sleep, I really don't feel good either. Sometimes I only sleep for three hours at night."

"What? How do you survive like this?" I asked.

"I sleep at the weekend to make up for it."

"Wow, that's not good. Why do you think you can't sleep during the week?"

"I don't know," she answered.

We finished our cigarettes and went back upstairs. Mo was watching me. The sight of him began to make me sick.

"Have a nice weekend," I said.

"See you Monday," Gausika replied.

"See you, Sophie," Vince said.

On the way home, I bought more drinks. I was aware that all of this was not good at all. My lack of sleep and my alcohol consumption began to mess me up slowly but surely, but I felt like I was a fly trapped in a spiderweb. Mo's mind games worked. He made me constantly think about him. An additional problem was that I didn't have a social circle. I had nothing to do at the weekend, and as Asiri had moved out, I had no one to talk to, which I would have needed to clear my thoughts. All I had was a job, which I hated, a single room in London and smoking breaks with Gausika. I was thinking about Mo for almost twenty-four hours. It was annoying, and it sucked all positive energy out of me. I had ignored Mo; I had talked to him, and I had sent him messages on Teams. None of it had worked. My sleep deprivation was health-damaging, and it affected my ability to perform well on the job.

The entire weekend was spent forming a plan to solve this dilemma. Quitting the job without having a new one was not an option, for I would not have been able to support myself anymore. Talking to Mo had proved to be pointless. In an act of desperation, I took inspiration from the movie 'How to lose a guy in ten days.' Andie had played a convincing part of a crazy, clingy woman in that movie, and Benjamin only had stayed with her because he had made a bet. Although it was risky, I plotted to drive Mo away with desperate, clingy and annoying messages. The problem was that I didn't want the whole office to consider me crazy, and at the same time, I couldn't tell anyone what I was planning to do because I had seen Vince reporting to Mo. "Of course, I could tell Gausika," I thought. As she used to have a crush on Mo, I wasn't sure whether I could trust her. I knew I needed a cover story, an excuse to act crazy with Mo. By Monday, the plan to put an end to Mo's mind games was formed inside my head.

At ten o'clock, I had a Zoom meeting. My team declared how much they anticipated coming to London next week. We discussed what we would be doing together during their visit. I looked forward to meeting them but felt the urgency to implement my plan as soon as possible. I was still on probation, and Iris would watch my performance closely. Therefore, I couldn't risk being deprived of sleep during their stay. The opportunity presented itself on Friday as Mo was again not in the office.

"I can't stop thinking about Mo," I said to Piri and Vince

in the afternoon.

"I thought you said you didn't want to go out with him," Vince said.

"Yeah, but I changed my mind." I replied. "I will text him right now."

"Don't do that," Piri replied.

"I don't want this to be over," I texted Mo on Teams.

"Oh, my god. I can't believe what I just texted. Look," I said.

"It can't get any more stupid," Piri replied.

Vince looked at the text.

"Delete it. There is a good chance that he hasn't seen the message yet," he said.

I took a deep breath. "It's showtime," I thought.

"Since my half-brother has died of a drug overdose, I am thinking how much you fuck up your life," I typed.

"Oh, my god. Don't send that," Piri said, but I pressed send anyway.

"Is that what happened? Your half-brother died?" Vince asked.

"Yes," I replied.

I forged crying but wasn't sure whether my performance had been credible or not. Vince and Piri, however, were deluded by it. It gave me no pleasure to lie to Piri, for I liked him very much. The possibility was there that Piri would inform Gausika should I have revealed the plan to him. There was a risk that Gausika could see that as an opportunity to win Mo for herself. I couldn't trust Vince anyway, for I had overheard him revealing private things about me to Mo.

"I know why you are doing this. You are grieving," Piri said.

"Yes, that must be it. It only happened two weeks ago."

"Let's go outside for a bit," Piri said.

I rolled a cigarette, and Piri and I, accompanied by Vince, went out for a smoke.

"I will make sure you get home alright," Piri said.

"No, this is not necessary," I replied.

"It is. We can't let you go home like this by yourself," Piri said firmly.

Vince looked awkward. It was clear that he didn't know what to say.

"OK," I said.

I was not entirely comfortable with Piri's offer to accompany me home, for I knew it would be very difficult to keep my lies up with a person I liked.

"Let's get some drinks. It's medicine," Piri said on the journey to my place.

"Sounds like a plan," I replied.

I got myself a couple of gin and tonic cans, and Piri bought a bottle of Whiskey.

"Do you want me to stay with you?" he asked when we had arrived at my place.

"Yeah, I think that would be good. But I don't want to talk about my half-brother. I am not ready for that yet," I replied, knowing I wouldn't be able to keep up this made-up story forever.

"No problem," he replied.

"Just don't try anything tonight," I said.

"Gausika would never forgive me if I would try anything with you, Sophie. So don't worry."

"You like Gausika. Don't you?"

"Yes, we have been friends for years."

"You know what I meant."

"I do. I am just not sure if she wants to. We kissed once, but then she acted like it was nothing. I think she is not ready for a relationship."

"Just give her time. I am sure she will come around."

Piri and I drank a lot that night. I avoided the subject of my half-brother and Mo. Piri was a very intelligent guy, and I knew that if I lied further, I probably would give myself away at some point. The next morning, we woke up early. Piri took a sip of the whisky.

"You drink in the morning?" I asked.

"Sometimes," he replied.

"And I thought that I was the one with the drinking

problem."

He laughed.

"I have to go now. I'm meeting Gausika later."

"Thanks for last night. I appreciate your company."

"You're not alone. We are always there for you," he replied.

We hugged each-other. I didn't feel good after he had left. I didn't have a bad conscience because I had lied to Mo. I knew that it had been necessary. But lying to everyone else was something I certainly was not proud of. The thought that my plan would work made me sleep like a baby, though.

Chapter 12

On Monday, I was in a state of agitation because I was going to meet my team for the first time and because I was apprehensive of Mo's reaction to my messages. I arrived at the office fifteen minutes early to ensure that I would be able to give my visitors a warm welcome. My team arrived at quarter past nine.

"Hi, Iris. Nice to finally meet you," I said.

"Hi, Sophie. Lovely to meet you too," she replied.

Iris was a short woman in her forties. She appeared to have a very friendly disposition, which soothed my apprehension.

"How was your journey here?" I asked.

"All went well," she replied.

I turned towards the others.

"Hi, Sophie. Finally, see you in person," Carsten said.

Carsten was tall and had already white hair. I got the impression that he was amiable.

"Likewise," I replied.

"Hi, Sophie. We will now be able to laugh about the planners together," Mimoun said.

"Something to look forward to," I replied.

Mimoun, who was from Morocco, always had amusing stories to tell about the employees of the German bank and never failed to entertain me. I saw Dylan walking towards us.

"Hi, welcome to the London office," he said to Iris.

"Thanks, Dylan."

"I will show you to your desks. Follow me, please."

"See you later," Mimoun said to me.

"Sophie, we will have a meeting in thirty minutes," Iris said.

"OK," I replied.

Once they were out of earshot, I turned myself towards Gausika.

"It's a bit awkward that they are here," I said.

"Yes, I can imagine that. It must be nice, though, to meet them finally."

"That's true, but usually nobody watched me when I was working. Now I will have people monitoring me every day."

"Yeah, that must be weird," she said.

Twenty-five minutes later, the meeting started. We

reviewed the program for the entire week and discussed the objectives of the gathering. I attempted to pay attention, although my thoughts were somewhere else. When I looked up, I caught sight of Mo. He was in the company of a co-worker. His face was distorted with rage. In response to the sight of me, he banged his fist against the meeting room's glass. My team-mates looked up. Shock paralyzed me for a brief moment, for I certainly would never have expected him to display violent behaviour in the presence of a manager. It required a good deal of determination, but I managed to regain control over my emotions. I followed the conversations as well as my mental state allowed me to. Two hours later, the meeting came to an end.

"I am going out for a cigarette," I said once we stepped out of the meeting room.

"Oh, you smoke? I am coming too," Mimoun said.

The awkward silence was hanging in the air on the way down.

"You're soon out of the probation period. Aren't you?" Mimoun said once we had lighted our cigarettes.

"Yes, provided, of course, I will pass it," I replied.

"You don't have to worry. You have done a great job so far. You will pass."

"I hope I will."

"You will. I know that Iris is very satisfied with your work, and so am I."

"I am happy to hear it."

"Do you have a boyfriend?" he asked.

"No, I am single," I answered.

"How come?"

"Well, I am not living in London that long, and I just haven't met anyone I like yet."

"Oh, I am sure you will meet someone soon."

"Thanks, Mimoun."

At twelve, I went out for lunch by myself as I was in need of some alone time. I bought a wrap and ate it behind the office building, where I was well hidden from the eyes of my co-workers. "I don't understand why Mo thinks he can act like that in an office and get away with it. I would never dare to bang against the glass while other employees have a meeting," I thought. What I couldn't figure out was why the managers didn't discipline him. Surely, behaviour like this was highly inappropriate and against company policy. At one, Iris, Carsten, and Mimoun came to my desk.

"Would you like to join us for lunch, Sophie?" Carsten asked.

"I already had lunch. I always have it early. Thanks for asking, though," I replied.

"Not to worry, Sophie. Today after work, we all will go to dinner together," he replied.

"I am looking forward to it. Enjoy your lunch," I replied.

"Thanks," Carsten said.

Fear came over me once they were out of sight. "My plan clearly wasn't well thought through," I reflected. I attempted to do some work but was interrupted every couple of minutes with thoughts about Mo's creepy behaviour. "Is he dangerous? Should I give him what he wants," I was asking myself. I could see that Gausika was watching me. She was a clever girl, and therefore, I was certain it wouldn't escape her notice that I appeared distracted. "Mo wants to have his ego satisfied. He wants to prove that he could have me if he wanted to," I considered. "If Mo won't leave me alone, I will give him what he wants. I will satisfy his ego, and I will make sure it will be the most annoying experience of his life," I concluded.

Later in the afternoon, I went out for a cigarette with Gausika. In order to make my cover story appear as plausible as possible, I repeated the tale of my half-brother's death.

"Yeah?" she asked.

I wasn't sure whether she suspected that I was not being honest or whether she had no empathy for the suffering of other people.

"Yes, he died of a drug-overdose," I replied.

"That's horrible. I am so sorry for your lose."

There was not an ounce of compassion in her tone of

voice. I knew I had to be on my guard with her. If the true purpose of my messages were revealed to Mo, he would be boiling with rage.

"Thanks, I just need time to grieve."

"Yeah, it will take time."

"Did you ever suffer a loss?" I asked.

"Yes, my grandmother died a couple of years back. It was really hard," she said.

"Oh, I am sorry."

"It's ok now," she replied.

We had finished our cigarettes and went back upstairs. Just as I sat down at my desk, Mimoun came over.

"Sophie, we have a reservation at an Italian restaurant for six o'clock," he said.

"Oh, great. I love Italian," I replied.

"Who doesn't?" he said.

I laughed. At quarter to six, we left the office together. There was little conversation on the way. We reached the restaurant after a ten minutes' walk.

"Reservation for CooperateEvent," Iris said to the waiter.

"Follow me, please," he replied.

I sat between Mimoun and Iris.

"Everything you order will be paid by the company," Iris said.

"Oh, great, I replied.

"Shall we start with a round of drinks?" Carsten asked.

"Sounds good to me," Iris replied.

I ordered a gin and tonic, and the others ordered a beer.

"Don't you drink alcohol?" Carsten asked.

"This is alcohol. Did you never have a gin and tonic before?" I asked.

"No, I drink beer," he replied.

"Sometimes I drink beer as well, but most of the time, it's gin and tonic," I said.

He nodded.

"You're Muslim. Aren't you?" I asked Mimoun.

"Yes, why?" he asked.

"I just wondered why you drink alcohol," I replied.

"I am sometimes Muslim," he answered.

I laughed. He laughed in return. I liked Mimoun as he was very sharp-witted. Although it had been a pleasant evening, I was relieved when the time came to say goodbye as I felt a great need to process the events of the day. After dinner, my team expressed the wish to go for a walk, but I was determined to go home. Therefore, I wished them a good night.

I refrained from consuming more alcohol that night, for I considered it unwise to attend work with a hangover the next day. Mo's behaviour certainly worried me, but I still managed to get some decent sleep. The following day, I woke up at seven. I dressed carefully because I wanted to make a good and decent impression while my team was in London. My outfit consisted of mom jeans, a white t-shirt and a black blazer. I looked again at how I had done at the beginning of my employment at CooperateEvent.

"How was the walk yesterday?" I asked Mimoun when they arrived.

"We went to a pub close to our hotel. That was our walk," he replied.

I laughed.

"I am sure it was good exercise," I said.

He grinned. My presence was required in meetings almost the entire day. On Wednesday, we got an email from Dylan. He informed us that we were allowed to finish work at three in the afternoon due to the match. It turned out that almost the entire office was going to be in the pub to watch the game. Gausika and I decided that we were going together. I informed Iris that I would meet them there. The first person I saw upon entrance was Mo. He had a very deranged look on his face.

"Oh shit," I said out loud.

"What is it?" Gausika asked.

"Let's smoke one before we go inside," I replied.

She nodded. We stepped outside and lit a cigarette.

"Mo is in there," I said.

"Just act like it is nothing. Can you do that?" Gausika replied.

I took a drag from my cigarette.

"It should be fine," I answered.

We went inside and ordered our drinks. Mo was no longer at the bar. It was the same pub where Mo and I had kissed. "What would you do without pleasant memories," I thought. Gausika and I joined my team. I hardly paid attention to the match. Apparently, neither did Mo. I saw him going out with a co-worker. "I need to know what is going on," I thought.

"I am going to the loo," I said.

"Do you want me to come with you?" Gausika asked.

"No, it is ok," I replied.

Instead of going to the toilet, I followed Mo outside. In order to ensure that I was able to hear every word he was saying, I sat down a short distance from him. I lighted a cigarette as it provided the perfect excuse for me to go after him.

"Sounds like she is complicated," the co-worker said to Mo.

I knew he was a new starter who had only worked at the company for a week. Mo appeared to have a real urge to debate the matter.

"No, I don't think she was complicated," Mo replied.

The co-worker nodded in response.

"I think I just will go home and process it," Mo added.

I went over to Mo.

"I am sorry," I said in order to inquire how Mo would react to an apology.

"It's fine," he shouted.

His tone had been again very hostile. He took his leave without saying another word. I went back inside and watched the rest of the match, but I was wondering what kind of game Mo was playing. He was in a relationship. I was certain of it because of the conversation I had overheard between Amange and Jennifer. Therefore, I couldn't understand Mo's need to talk about me and the situation.

England lost that night. The spirit of most pub visitors was grievously dampened. My team and Gausika left once the match had finished. I took another drink and stepped outside for a smoke, joining in a conversation with two of my co-workers. One was called Oscar, and the other one was called Owen. I had never talked to them before, but they seemed amiable and fun. All of a sudden, a fight broke out. Oscar and Owen wanted to participate in it, but I made great effort to pull them away from the scene.

"Let me go back there," Owen said very loud.

"No, you could get into serious trouble," I replied, but Owen made again an attempt to go back.

"Give me a hand," I demanded from Oscar.

In the end, Oscar and I managed to drag Owen away.

"I wanted to help my friends," Owen said.

"Let's go for another drink somewhere," Oscar said.

"Yeah, let's get some cans," I replied.

We bought some drinks in a shop in the train station, which we drank in the underground.

"James is your brother. Isn't he?" I said to Oscar.

"He is. How do you know that?" he asked.

"Gausika, the Sri Lankan girl, told me," I replied.

"James has left the company," he said.

"Why?" I asked.

"He just wasn't really happy at the company anymore," Oscar answered.

"I think your brother used to have a crush on me," I said to Oscar.

"I am certain that he did. But you know he and Mo are really good friends. James would never do anything to upset Mo," Oscar replied.

I was furious.

"I see," I answered.

"Have a good night," I said to them just before I went out two stops later.

"See you tomorrow," Oscar and Owen replied.

Rage took control of me by the time I arrived at home. If Oscar had been truthful, then the gorgeous James used to be smitten with me, but he never had made a move because of that damn idiot Mo. Although I knew that there was something wrong with Mo and although I knew that Mo was capable of violent behaviour, I wanted to get back at him for this. Why did Oscar anyway know about this? And why on earth had James been worried about upsetting Mo? It would have been vastly unwise to retaliate before my team's departure. I was well aware of it, and therefore, I decided to wait.

CHAPTER 13

The next day, I encountered Oscar and Owen outside when I went out for a smoke. Brigitta did stand very close by with her friend Sita. I didn't escape my notice that she was watching me.

"Hi," I said.

"Hi," Oscar replied.

"Wild night yesterday. Wasn't it?" I said.

"You can say that," Oscar replied.

"You should have let me go back and help my friends," Owen replied.

"She got you out of a very tight spot yesterday. You owe her big time," Oscar replied.

"Hmmm," Owen let out.

"You might want to come on a double date with me and Owen sometime?" Oscar asked.

I looked at Brigitta and noticed with great pleasure that she looked uncomfortable.

"We can do that one of these days," I replied.

"Great," Oscar said.

The rest of the week past smoothly, and on Friday evening, I farewelled Iris and the rest of my team. Once I arrived home that evening, I took action to make Mo regret the day he had decided to deceive and hassle me. Although retaliation was certainly an objective of mine, my peace of mind was the ultimate long-term goal. In order to avoid being labelled as crazy, I used again the tale of my dead half-brother. Surely, everyone was going to see that I was just grieving.

"I just watched Collateral Beauty. It's about a guy who lost his daughter. Then, he gets visited by love, time and death. They show him the meaning of life. It's so beautiful and sad. You should watch it. It reminds me so much of my half-brother's death." I pressed send.

"One text isn't enough. It must get annoying," I thought.

"I am just sitting at home and drinking. It's so hard for me to deal with it. He died so young. I feel like I have lost control over myself." I pressed send.

"It makes you really think about life when you lose a family member of a drug overdose. Love, friendship and family are the most important things in life." I pressed send again.

While smoking outside, I wondered how Mo would perceive and react to those messages. When I got back, I got a message from him.

"Stop texting me. This is absolutely unacceptable. Go out and enjoy your life."

Mo didn't want to be bothered with someone's troubles. This much was obvious. I thought that I would keep that in mind. Although I expected Mo to cease his attempt to pursue me, I was by no means certain of it as it was now quite obvious that Mo had zero empathy. Most people would show compassion towards a person who has suffered a loss. Not him.

On Saturday morning, I got a text from Piri. He asked me to come to his place to hang out with him and his friend. The invitation was most welcome, for I had a great need to talk about Mo and clear my head. Piri lived in the middle of nowhere. It took me almost two hours to get to his place. I knocked on his door, and one minute later, Piri opened the door.

"Hi, Sophie," he said with a huge smile.

"Hi, Piri."

"Come on in."

"Do you live here by yourself?" I asked while looking around curiously.

"No, I live here with my parents."

"Nice."

I knew that Sri Lankan people were family people, and therefore, it didn't surprise me that Piri shared a place with his parents. A short guy with ginger hair and bad acne came walking towards us.

"Sophie, this is Henry," Piri said.

"Hi, Henry. It's nice to meet you."

"Likewise, Sophie."

We went into the garden as Piri was aware that I wanted to smoke a cigarette. I told him I let my anger out on Mo without going into the details.

"Good for you, Sophie. Why don't you tell Henry about it as well?" he said.

"Oh, I wouldn't wish to bother him with that story," I replied.

"I would like to hear about it," Henry said.

I recounted the entire story, or most of it. Once I told Henry that Mo had smashed the computer mouse on the table, kicked open the door in the office and banged his fist against the glass, he made a weird noise.

"Right, stay away from him. Cut every communication and never talk to him again. This guy is a total psychopath. If he is willing to do something like this in public, imagine what he would be willing to do behind closed doors," he said.

I was fully aware that Henry was right, but that didn't change anything about the fact that I was still angry with Mo.

"Yeah, you are probably right," I said.

"I am. Trust me. I got a feeling for this kind of thing," he said.

"Don't you think it a display of strength?" Piri asked.

"No, I don't. There is something very wrong with that guy," Henry replied.

Piri and I nodded. We both knew that Henry was right, but who the hell would be happy about the revelation that a psychopath was working in the same office? The rest of the afternoon we spent watching movies. Later, Piri cooked for us.

"My god. The Sri Lankan food is really the best food ever," I said.

"Thanks, Sophie," he said with a huge smile.

Piri was really an incredibly nice guy, but somehow, I wasn't able to enjoy his company the way I could have had, when I wouldn't have been that concerned about Mo's creepy behaviour. I was feeling guilty about it when I arrived at home. "I have good people in my life, but I am thinking about a psychopath. I wish I could stop thinking about him, and I wish I would never have met Mo. My time at CooperateEvent would have been so different when he hadn't worked there," I thought while lying in bed.

On Monday at ten in the morning, Mo walked past my desk with Amange beside him.

"She told me that she loves me, and the good thing is that she already knows about the situation," Mo said to Amange.

"That's great," Amange replied.

It was most convenient that Mo had chosen precisely the moment to inform Amange about the love declaration he had received.

"So, he finally went public with his relationship," I thought. Hate grew inside my heart. He had tried to deceive me more than once and only had made his relationship official because he thought that it would hurt my feelings to see him with another woman. It was that hate that tempted me to retaliate and humiliate Mo again. Although it was imprudent, I texted Mo the following Saturday. "I am sorry when I did hurt your feelings. I was grieving because of the death of my half-brother. It was nothing personal."

Mo didn't disappoint. On Monday, I met him at the entrance to the office when I was about to walk out with Gausika.

"Hi, Sophie," he said.

I didn't reply. Gausika didn't say anything to him either. Mo had acted the way I had expected him to. He had made an attempt to prove that he would be able to win my heart like it was a trophy. I was delighted that I had succeeded in degrading him by not responding to his greeting.

"I started to apply for some graphic design jobs," I told Gausika when we were smoking outside.

"Really? Have you already heard anything back?" she asked.

"Not yet. But I will keep trying. What about you? Don't you want to work as a designer," I asked her.

"I would love to. But I gave up on it a long time ago. I don't think it will ever happen to me," she replied.

In the elevator, I thought that Mo must be really simple-minded. A girl with romantic feelings for a man would never send such messages and surely would reply when the man of her dreams would say hello. Just when we came back from the smoking break, I saw Mo talking to Brigitta.

"But you said he would see me now," she told Amange when Mo walked away.

"I had no idea. Really," Amange replied.

"How convenient to talk about this within my earshot," I thought. On Friday, I overheard Mo talking about me.

"And all this just to get Sophie back," a co-worker said to him.

"No, I had no idea that her half-brother had died. Honestly," Mo replied.

It was a highly inappropriate conversation, especially when I considered that they talked about in a short distance from my desk. Piri came over in precisely that moment.

"We are going for a drink after work. Are you coming too, Sophie?" he asked.

"Sure, why not?" I replied.

At half past five, Vince, Gausika, Piri, and I left the office. On the way, I told the others about Mo's inappropriate gossip about me.

"You know how many people in the office hate him?" Piri asked.

"No, I don't," I replied.

"A lot. Ugne hates him, Gausika hates him, I hate him, and about half the office hates him," Piri replied.

Vince nodded.

"The other day, he talked shit to me. I told him he shouldn't speak to me like this," Piri added.

"He is a dickhead," Vince added.

"You know what? I am going back to the office and tell him my opinion," I said.

"Don't do that," Gausika replied.

"No, I am going. I will be straight back," I said.

The others made no further attempt to prevent me from going. Mo walked out of the office precisely when I had reached the building.

"You know I really hate you. You talk about me within my earshot and even talk about my half-brother's death. Do you have actually any idea how hard it is to lose a family member?" I said to him.

Mo laughed. It was outrageous. I lost control of myself and punched him on the arm.

"Don't hit or touch me," he said.

"I hardly even touched you," I replied.

"You are crazy. Get away from me," he said.

He tried to escape, but I chased after him. He got away from me when he stepped into a bus. In a state of fury, I walked back to the pub. He had literally laughed about the death of a family member. "How sick is this," I thought.

"Where have you been?" Piri asked.

"I just had a little chat with Mo. I told him that I hated him and that he should stop talking shit about me. I told him that I was going through a very difficult time because of my half-brother's death. Then he laughed, and I did punch him," I said.

"Did anyone see you? Were there any cameras?" Vince asked.

"No cameras and nobody from the office saw it," I replied.

"Then you should be good," Vince said.

"Well done, Sophie. I am so proud of you. I would love to punch him myself," Piri said.

"I think it would be better, Sophie, if you would do

something like this sober. Mo would take you way more seriously then," Gausika said.

"You think?" I replied sarcastically.

On Monday, most employees of CooperateEvent were at an event which lasted four days. I had too much work to do, and therefore, I remained in the office. "Four days without Mo. Sounds like heaven to me," I thought while enjoying the quiet. On Friday we had a big meeting, which the company's CEO did attend. From my desk, I observed Brigitta handing Mo her scarf. "So, they made their relationship official and no longer try to deceive people," I thought. Shortly afterwards, I overheard John talking about it.

"I wonder why Mo is with Brigitta and why he made his relationship with her public now. She is the ugliest woman in the company," he said.

"Shh, someone could hear you. I wouldn't mess with them," his friend Daniel replied. "Brigitta is really ugly and stupid. Mo very much deserves her," I thought cheerfully. It was my obligation to participate in the meeting, but I would have preferred to do my work. For my peace of mind, I chose a seat far away from Mo. Gausika had a call and, therefore, couldn't attend. "Lucky her," I thought. The meeting was very dull. After about ten minutes, the CEO started staring at me. During his entire speech, he only looked at me. "What kind of company is this?" I thought. My frustration had reached a new high. I didn't work as a graphic designer; I had to deal every day with that idiot Mo. I was only able to afford a small room in London, and now the CEO was harassing me with inappropriate behaviour. The other employees noticed, of course. Dylan looked very uncomfortable, but Mo shouted, 'He is looking at Sophie.' Brigitta's face was distorted with jealousy. This made her look even more ill-favoured. I walked out and pretended that I had to go to the toilet while I took my cigarettes and escaped by using the fire exit. "This is unbelievable," I thought while I was smoking outside.

Only the prospect of my horse-riding holiday in Morocco, which I had booked two weeks ago, improved my mood. The trip was expensive, but it was worth it, for it was of important to get away from all this drama. After a fifteen minutes break, I returned to the office and endured the rest of the meeting. We were informed that we all would go to a pub later and that the drinks would be on the company.

"Are you coming too?" I asked Gausika once the meeting was over.

"I never say no to free drinks," she replied.

"Great," I replied.

"I think Mo goes out with Brigitta," I said a little later.

"Oh, Brigi. I think she must be a bit of a slut. She lives with her boyfriend in Hampstead. He is Muslim, too," Vince replied.

I knew from then on, that Vince had known about Mo's relationship with Brigitta and asked myself if Gausika had known as well. "Can I trust anyone?" I asked myself. "Why would Vince support Mo?" I thought furiously. At five, Gausika, Vince, Piri, and I left the office together. Once we arrived at the pub, I ordered two gin and tonics.

"Thirsty?" Piri asked.

"Oh, you have no idea," I replied.

Sara joined our table. We told her about the story with Mo.

"She did actually hit him," Piri said to Sara.

"No way," she replied.

"Trust me. He had it coming," I declared.

"Yes, he did, and the best part is that he can't do anything about it. He is Muslim and was supposed to hit you back, but if he does, then he will get fired," Piri said.

Brigitta was sitting opposite us and was able to hear every word.

"Look, there he is," Piri said.

I looked up and saw Mo walking towards Brigitta.

"I was just looking around. I hope it won't get awkward between us," I heard him say to her.

Later, I saw them in the pub together. She was smiling, and I was outraged. Brigitta would have been more upset if

Mo really had ended his relationship with her. "They are really sick," I thought when I went to the toilet. I knew why Mo had pretended to break up with Brigitta. The CEO had been staring at me during the entire meeting. Every employee had noticed that which meant they would all consider me unusually beautiful. "Mo will try to chase me again. I can't let that happen," I thought. In an attempt to calm myself, I got really drunk that night. When I arrived at my place, the hate inside my heart took the upper hand.

"I heard you date girls who are in a relationship. You are really the last piece of shit. You stupid Muslim," I texted Mo on Teams and pressed send.

On Saturday, I woke up at eight in the morning and was very hangover. I knew that Mo would back off now and that he never would try to chase me again. But I was asking myself if I had gone too far.

CHAPTER 14

In the afternoon, I started packing. My veins pulsed with anticipatory excitement. I would spend an entire week in Agadir riding horses. Morocco could be very warm during the day and very cold in the evenings. Therefore, I packed lots of t-shirts and a couple of warm jumpers. The next day, I took the flight from London Heathrow airport at six in the evening. There was no direct flight from London to Agadir, so I had to change to Casablanca. The journey went surprisingly smoothly when I considered my general bad luck. When I arrived in Agadir, I felt the life coming back to me. I felt free, and Mo was forgotten. A bus picked me up at one in the morning. One hour later, I arrived at the horse range. Although I was very tired, I felt invigorated by the beauty of the place. Not long after I had stepped out of the bus, someone came to assist me with my luggage. I was guided to my room, which was very spacious. The bed was huge, and I very much looked forward to sleeping in it.

"Breakfast will be served at half past seven. At nine, you will get your horse," he said to me.

"Sounds great. Thanks," I replied.

I slept like I had never slept before. All my troubles were far away, and I felt like I had been reborn. My excitement woke me up at half past six the next morning. I got quickly dressed and went outside. It was breathtaking. There were exotic flowers everywhere. The paddocks were in front of me, and the Atlantic Ocean was behind me. I smoked a cigarette and then went to the stables to pet the horses. A stable lad took a beautiful white Arabian stallion out of his box.

"Hi," I said.

He smiled but didn't reply. I thought he probably didn't speak English, as French was the second language in Morocco. The horse was stunning. I hoped that I would get a chance to ride him. At half past seven, I went into the breakfast room, where a group of French-speaking girls joined me. My French wasn't great, and therefore, a real conversation wasn't possible. The breakfast consisted of toast, ham, jams and fresh fruits. At home, I never ate breakfast, but in Agadir, I really ate heartily. After breakfast, I took my amazing coffee outside and smoked a cigarette while enjoying the breath-taking view. It was magical. Ten minutes later, I went back to my room and changed into my riding clothes. Outside, a stable lad came towards me.

"Hi, are you Sophie?" he asked.

"I am," I replied.

"Nice to meet you. I am Mohamed. You will be riding with me," he said.

"It somehow doesn't bother me that he has the same name as the weirdo back home," I thought.

"Hi, Mohamed."

"Call me Mo."

"Mo, it is."

"Are you a good rider?" Mo asked.

"I am. I used to ride racehorses in Ireland."

"Racehorses? Cool. So, you will want a very fast horse then."

"Yes, the best you got."

He laughed.

"I just have the horse for you," he said.

He walked away, and I followed him. He showed me a beautiful chestnut Arabian-Berber horse I would be riding during my stay.

"He is gorgeous," I said.

"Isn't he? Do you need help tacking up Sophie?" Mo asked.

"No, I think I will be fine. Thanks."

"You're a tough one. Cool. I'll show you the tack room," he replied.

It was most bizarre. Mo had done me wrong when he had tried to deceive me, but none of that affected my perception of the people in Morocco and even someone who shared his name. I was proud of myself that I didn't let one bad experience turn me into a racist. I tacked up my horse and then led him out to the paddock.

"Nice job, Sophie," Mo said.

"Shukran," I replied.

"Do you speak Arabic?" he asked.

"No, I just know that word."

"Well, that was very good."

"Thanks," I said.

"You can get up on the horse from the bucket," he said.

"It's ok. I got it," I replied.

I took the reins into my hands and jumped up smoothly from the ground.

"I have never seen a woman do that," he said.

I just smiled in response. Once I was on the horse, I felt like I was home. Horses have had that effect on me since I was a child.

"Just walk him a bit. I go and get my horse," Mo said.

Ten minutes later, we were on the way. Amazing was the

word that described the beauty of nature that I had the pleasure of seeing. Morocco was really as pretty as a picture. There was so much variety in the landscape, and the people we met along the way were warm and amiable. I considered the people in Morocco to be liberal and progressive in their attitude.

"Why don't the women wear burkas?" I asked Mo while we passed a couple of Muslim women.

"They can if they want to, but they don't have to. The women in this country are free," he replied.

I very much approve of that. The Moroccans were religious but thought and decided for themselves. I always considered the enforcement of the burka as a form of slavery. Therefore, I thought that many Muslim countries could take a leaf out of Morocco's book. Mo was impressed with my riding skills. Therefore, we cantered a lot more than he would have done with a beginner. My horse was very fast, but not as speedy as Mo's horse.

"Yalla," Mo said when we arrived at the beach.

"What does that mean?" I asked.

"It means let's go," he replied.

"Yalla," I said.

My horse clearly listened, for I felt his excitement. Mo's horse started to canter. I gave mine the heels, and off we went.

"This is amazing," I screamed.

Mo laughed. I went into the racing position as we were galloping now. The experience made me feel so alive. Since I started at CooperateEvent, I have only worked and been involved in drama. In Morocco, I was living.

"You are a great rider," Mo said.

"Shukran," I replied.

Twenty minutes later, we were back at the stables. I tacked up my horse and then looked for Mo.

"I had an exciting time. Thank you so much for today," I said.

"You are very welcome, Sophie," he replied.

I wasn't tired. As a matter of fact, I could have stayed on the horse all day. Back in my room, I reflected on the events of the day and thought that only someone like Mo from England interpreted the Islam the way he wanted and gave it a bad reputation.

I smelled like a horse, and therefore, I immediately took a shower. The warm water dripped down my body, and I felt every muscle relax. It was a bit windy. Therefore, I changed into some sweatpants and a t-shirt afterwards. A staircase was leading up to the roof of my bungalow. Up there, I let the sun warm my face, and the breath-taking view over the ocean astounded me. I felt so at peace with myself and my environment. I lingered on the roof until the sunset and then went down to the dining room. All the girls wore sweatpants like me. It felt a bit like a pyjama party. The food was beyond delicious. The meat was so juicy, and the plumbs so sweet. I considered the Moroccan cuisine as the best kitchen ever. The seven hours of riding had exhausted me greatly, and therefore, I went to bed early.

Every day, we rode out in the morning, came back for lunch and then went again in the afternoon. It was every time a different trail. I couldn't converse much with the other girls on the farm because they just spoke French. Therefore, it was a bit lonely sometimes in the evenings. On Thursday, it started raining very heavily. "This is just my luck. It rains about every four years in Morocco and has to rain precisely when I am there on a holiday," I thought. Morocco was not equipped to deal with this kind of weather. Soon, I had a swimming pool in my room, and we couldn't ride out either. It was cold, wet and uncomfortable. Most of us took shelter in the dining room, which turned out to be the most waterproof. The electricity wasn't working anymore either. The only light we had came from candles. It would have been romantic if not everything would have been this wet. In order to distract myself, I went out smoking a lot that day. I took a book with me but felt too uncomfortable to read. Sleeping that night was very difficult as I had weird dreams about Mo.

The next day, the sun was out again, and everything

started to dry. It was a huge relief because I feared it would rain for the rest of my holiday. The woman who owned the farm assured me at breakfast that I could go riding on Sunday morning if I wanted to. I was very grateful that she gave me the chance to make up for the missed ride from the previous day. The guide and I went out with the horses at ten in the morning and rode for two hours. Just when we arrived at the beach, we saw four scooters coming our way. My horse became very nervous and rose into the air. I stayed calm and managed to keep it under control.

"That was very good. You know how to stay relaxed in a difficult situation," Mo said.

"Thanks," I replied.

"Yalla Yalla," he said.

We cantered on and went a bit faster this time. Sunday came too soon. I rode out in the morning, wishing that it would never end. At twelve, I was served a delicious lunch. I ate heartily, for I knew the food back home wouldn't be as delightful as the food in Morocco. Afterwards, I took a shower and packed all my stuff together. At six in the evening, the bus picked me up to take me to the airport.

"Take care of yourself, Sophie. You are welcome here anytime you want to come back," Mo said when it was time to say goodbye.

"I will most definitely come back here. Thanks again, Mo.

I had an amazing time riding out with you," I responded.

I was very sad to leave and was devastated because I had to return to the office on Tuesday. I dreaded what would await me there. The journey home went smoothly, and the scenes of my adventures played inside my head like in a movie. I arrived on Monday morning at Heathrow Airport. By the time I got home, I was absolutely exhausted. "It sucks that I have to return to this living hell tomorrow," I thought while unpacking my luggage.

CHAPTER 15

The holiday greatly benefited my well-being. I felt mentally a lot stronger, healthier and untroubled. Physically, I was more attractive, for my body had been firmed during my riding sessions, and my skin had a beautiful glowing tint. After I had dressed, I enjoyed my reflection in the mirror. Confident, I made myself on the way. At five to nine, I arrived at the office. I drank my soya cappuccino and smoked a cigarette before I went in. Mo arrived two minutes after me. He looked enraged at the sight of me. The front door didn't open, so he had to use the other one close to where I stood. It was of little matter to me that Mo was angry. As a matter of fact, I thought it served him well. He took the stairs, and I took the elevator.

"Welcome back," Gausika said.

"Thanks," I replied.

"How was your trip?" Vince asked.

"It was truly amazing," I answered with a huge smile.

"I can see that. You look great," Gausika said.

"Thanks," I beamed.

"This is Aisha. She started here when you were away," Gausika said, pointing to the girl next to Vince.

"Nice to meet you. I heard a lot about you," Aisha declared.

"Don't worry. People exaggerate," I said.

"They were only saying good things about you," she said.

"Ha, sure. I go and get myself another coffee," I replied.

I went into the kitchen, where I encountered Mo.

"Guys, I made up my mind," he announced loudly and clearly to one of his friends.

I wasn't acquainted with the context of that conversation and was, therefore, indifferent to it. When I was back at my desk, I got a Teams message from Iris. She had inquired after my holiday.

"She is nice looking," I heard Mo say.

I noticed that he was watching me. "Oh, my god. When will this drama ever be over," I thought. I observed that Brigitta went over to Mo's desk.

"He is looking at Sophie," she shouted so loud that the entire office could hear her. "She looks shit," she screeched when she didn't get a reply.

Brigitta's remark about my appearance pleased Mo, for he had a huge smirk on his face.

I became aware that the story with Mo was far from being over. Later in the day, I went out for a smoke by myself and encountered Brigitta. I made sure that there was enough space between us. Just when I had lighted my cigarette, I saw Mo walking down the stairs through the windows of the office building. When he saw me, he started smiling. Outside, he joined Brigitta. I felt uncomfortable in their presence and, therefore, finished my cigarette quickly. I walked upstairs. Mo and Brigitta had apparently taken the elevator, for they arrived on the third floor at the same time as me.

"Don't worry. We will get rid of Sophie," he said just when we had entered the office.

His remark certainly hadn't made me feel good, for I had learnt that Mo's threats should not be underestimated. Worse than that, I overheard other employees gossip about me as well. Gausika and Vince were acting differently, too. Although they had greeted me in a friendly manner, their behaviour towards me was more reserved. "Mo must have shown the text, which I sent him before the holiday, to everyone in the office," I concluded. The purpose of those messages had been to put an end to Mo's mind games and to achieve my peace of mind. I never had considered for one moment how I would feel when every employee of

CooperateEvent would oppose me. At that moment, I was asking myself if I could have resolved the problem in a more civilized manner. I concluded that my actions and messages, although not fine, had been necessary. Ignoring Mo had not been an option, for Mo's mind games had deprived me of my sleep. Talking to him had proved to be pointless. In other words, any mature behaviour towards Mo was futile as it was obvious that he had aimed to play a game. "What is the worst that he can do? I will stay at the company a little longer and then get a graphic design job. The others will stop talking about it after a while," I thought.

The next day, it became apparent that Mo meant business and that he got support. I observed Amange approaching Ugne.

"We have to get rid of Sophie. It's just really awkward to have her here, but I can't be bothered. So, find a way, will you," he said to her.

It had not been a question. Amange had commanded it. I felt very troubled and highly distressed. My good mood and peace of mind had gone out in smoke. Two hours later, I went out with Gausika for a smoke and encountered Amange.

"They want to get rid of me because of the things I texted Mo," I told Gausika loud enough that Amange could hear me.

"Never let someone make you feel this way. You had a right to tell Mo your opinion," Gausika replied in a low voice.

Amange gazed over his shoulder. He looked a bit uncomfortable, which pleased me. I had the feeling that Gausika genuinely meant what she had said, but I also observed that she was discomfited with the situation. Later in the day, Gausika and Vince talked over my head.

"She asked me why I was still talking to Sophie like this. But I don't care what people will say. I have no problem with Sophie," Vince said to Gausika without bothering to keep his voice down.

I knew who she was. They were talking about Brigitta. I was aware that I should have said something to defend myself, but something was holding me back.

"It's best to let grass grow over the situation," I thought. Every day, however, it became apparent that it only would get worse. On Friday, I overheard a co-worker say that I was a racist. I was outraged because I certainly wasn't a racist. "How can they think that? I only texted Mo that he was a stupid Muslim because I was angry. Every idiot should be able to see that and also know that Mo deserved it," I thought furiously. It was hell in the office, and it was hell at home. A new tenant had moved in and inhabited Asiri's old room. He snored, and the walls were very thin. Therefore, I was once more deprived of my sleep. I decided to look for another room. It was a priority of mine as I was mentally and physically exhausted. It would have been best to end my employment with CooperateEvent. Due to a lack of resources and support, it was, however, impossible. I felt like I was trapped in a cage while everyone was watching me through the bars. Overhearing people gossiping about me distressed me greatly. I knew that I wasn't a racist, and I knew that Mo had tried to deceive me. The problem was that nobody else was aware of the truth.

In order to cope with my emotions, I consumed alcohol on a regular basis. The search for a new room provided some distraction and a small amount of hope. After a couple of days, I saw a room advertised, which appealed to me. I gave the woman who had posted the room a call. We scheduled a viewing for the following Thursday at half past six. Meanwhile, my job became a daily torture.

"Why is she still here?" I heard Brigitta scream at Amange on Monday morning.

The worst part was that she had been standing close to Dylan when she had shouted. I wondered why the management tolerated such behaviour. The messages which I had sent Mo had been rude. I was well aware of it. In my opinion, my behaviour towards Mo was justified, for his true intentions had been cruel. Although the consequences of those messages were severe, I didn't feel ashamed or guilty. I only had defended myself, and the knowledge helped me stand my ground.

On Thursday, I left the office at five. I arrived way too early at the Arnos Grove station. I was famished, and therefore, I went into the closest pub and ordered a steak, gin, and tonic. At half past six, I arrived at the house. I rang the bell, but nobody opened the door. "Hopefully she didn't forget," I thought. I gave the woman a call. After two minutes, she answered.

"Hi, it's Sophie. I am outside the house," I said.

"Hi, Sophie. Apologizes. I didn't hear the bell. I am coming out now."

One minute later, she opened the door.

"Welcome, I am Nathalie."

"Nice to meet you."

"Come on in. I will show you the house."

I followed her inside. The house was nice but not very tidy. She showed me first the living room, where a very handsome young man was sitting on the couch without a shirt on.

"This is my son, Josh," she said.

"Nice to meet you," I said.

"Likewise," he replied.

I had to grin. Nathalie had apparently noticed, for she said, 'Josh. You might want to put on a t-shirt.' He had a trained body, and I got the impression that he had no objections to showing it to everyone.

"OK," Josh replied.

"Come on. I will show you the kitchen," she said to me.

The kitchen was big but a total mess.

"Sorry, I came home late from work and didn't have a chance to clean before you arrived," she said.

"No problem."

Josh relocated himself to the dining table.

"Are you a student?" I asked.

"No, I am a professional tennis player. I most of the time away at tournaments."

"Oh, cool."

"Do you play tennis?" he inquired.

"No, I have never tried it."

"I will show you the room now," Nathalie said firmly.

Nathalie gave the impression that she didn't wish me to talk to Josh. "I wonder why that is," I thought. The room was big and looked very comfortable. Overall, Nathalie's house appeared to be a lot more pleasant than my current place.

"It's nice. I think I would like to take it."

"Good, when would you like to move in?"

"I could move in two weeks."

"Sounds good to me," she answered.

"Just don't give the room to somebody else," I requested.

"Don't worry. You seem like a very nice girl. I am more than happy to give you the room."

"Great, can you send me your bank details via email?" I asked.

"Sure, will do."

"Great, thanks. I am looking forward to the move," I said.

"Me too," Nathalie replied.

The prospect of the move made me feel slightly more optimistic. My hopefulness was, unfortunately, of short duration. On Friday, Ugne found a way to make me very uncomfortable in the office. The cold draft of the air conditioner caused me discomfort and severe pain in the neck and shoulders. Ugne was well aware of it, for I had complained about it several times. Apparently, she had given the order to turn the air conditioner up in the area where I was sitting. It was freezing cold. My shoulders contracted to such an extent that I was in unimaginable pain. I had to sit at my desk with a winter coat, scarf and hat.

"Take off that hat, Sophie. You look ridiculous," Vince demanded.

"I am freezing," I hissed back at him.

Brigitta, who apparently had heard me, laughed cheerfully. Her laugh was as silly as herself. It infuriated me. "This is such a stupid bitch," I thought. I did my best to hide my anger because I didn't want to satisfy her. Two weeks later, I moved. On Saturday morning, I took an Uber to Nathalie's house. Upon arrival, the driver helped to unload all my baggage.

"Thanks," I said.

"You're welcome. Take care of yourself," he replied.

I rang the bell. Nathalie opened the door.

"Welcome, Sophie."

"Hi, Nathalie."

"Do you need help with your stuff?"

"That would be great. Thanks."

"No problem."

Fifteen minutes later, we had moved everything into my new room. Afterwards, I went into the kitchen, where I met Josh.

"Oh, hello. I am surprised to see you here. I thought you said you would be away," I said.

"I am flying on Monday," he grumbled.

"Oh, nice. Where are you going?" I wondered.

"Spain."

"Cool."

"Yes," he replied. "Maman, can you please make me a sandwich?" he asked Nathalie.

"Give me a minute," she replied.

Josh was apparently a bit mollycoddled. "He must be about twenty-three years old and still asks his mother to make him a sandwich. What a spoiled brat," I thought. I made myself a glass of water and went back into my room, where I started unpacking. Later in the day, I walked to the closest store to buy groceries. When I came back, I saw Nathalie in the living room, kneeling in front of a Buddha. She was chanting. She looked up when she noticed me but didn't say anything. I went into the kitchen, which was again a mess. Nathalie approached me while I was unpacking my grocery bags.

"I bet you ask yourself what it was that I have been doing," she said.

"I do indeed."

"It's called nam myoho renge kyo. It's a form of Buddhism."

"Nice."

"You might want to chant with me sometimes. It's very good for you as it clears your karma."

"Sure, maybe."

I wasn't too enthusiastic about it, but I thought it couldn't hurt to try it.

CHAPTER 16

The move had exhausted me greatly. Therefore, I slept most of the day on Sunday. For the rest of my time, I used to watch TV while eating snacks. I was somehow able to relax, although I dreaded the next day.

"Do you come out for a cigarette?" I asked Gausika at ten on Monday morning.

"Sure, give me a minute. I have to finish that email. It won't take me long."

I rolled a cigarette and then waited for her. Five minutes later, we were standing outside.

"How is the new house?" she asked.

"It's very nice. The room is very big, and we even have a garden."

"Sounds good. I would like to move myself. It's so awkward in my place. Nobody talks. When I go into the kitchen, my housemate doesn't even say hello."

"Sounds horrible. You should defo move."

"I am trying. But I am still in debt. The people at my last work place were horrible. I quit my job and left without even saying goodbye. I had to work in Superdrug and borrowed money from a lot of people. I am still ten thousand pounds in debt."

"Wow, that is a lot."

"Yes, every month, I pay about six hundred back. Then I just got enough money left for food, rent and transport."

"That must be tough. I still owe my sister a thousand pounds."

"Thousand pounds is not that much," she replied.

"True, but it is still uncomfortable. I don't really want to stay at CooperateEvent, but I have to because otherwise I wouldn't be able to pay the rent."

She nodded, but it was obvious that she considered her situation as way more grievous.

"Aren't you cold in the office?" I interrogated her on the way upstairs.

"No, I am fine with it," she replied.

The freezing cold draft from the air conditioner became unbearable for me, and therefore, I wasn't quite able to comprehend why nobody else complaint about it.

"Are you cold?" I asked Aisha once I had sat down.

"Yes, I am freezing. My neck starts to get stiff," she replied.

"Something is wrong with the two of you. I am hot," Vince said.

"There is something wrong with you and not us," I snapped.

I noticed that Mo was watching me. It was no mystery why he was observing me. He wanted to inquire if he was able to pick something up that he could use as a weapon against me.

"Do you want to come for a drink after work?" I asked Gausika.

"Sorry, I got plans," she replied.

"She is using you as a smoking buddy. She doesn't really want to be your friend," Vince exclaimed so loud that everyone was able to hear him.

This was so humiliating and hurtful. Gausika looked uncomfortable but didn't respond.

"Is this true?" I asked.

"No," she retorted defensively.

The next day, Gausika asked me if I wanted to join her and Aisha outside for a cigarette.

"No, I am good," I replied.

"OK," she said.

Upon their return, I went out for a smoke by myself.

Vince's comment made me feel very resentful towards Gausika. I preferred not to talk or spend time with her anymore.

"Can we talk?" she asked just around lunch time.

"Fine," I snapped, fully aware that she could hear my resentment in my tone of voice.

"What's going on?" she asked once we had lighted our cigarettes.

"I don't want to be used," I replied.

"You can't take Vince seriously. Honestly, I like you just the way you are, and I am not using you as a smoking buddy."

"Really?"

"Yes, I am not lying to you."

"Well, apparently, the whole office wants to get rid of me because of what I texted Mo. Why not you?"

"Is that what you think? That we would side with Mo? Most of us don't like him."

At this moment, Piri came out.

"Is everything ok?" he asked.

"We were talking about what Vince said to Sophie. She thinks that we would side with Mo."

"Don't be silly. First of all, Vince always talks bullshit. Second. We don't like Mo. Remember," he said.

I considered for a brief moment to be entirely sincere with

them. Being honest would have involved admitting that I had lied to them, as well as Mo, and I didn't feel comfortable with that. The memory of Mo's display of violence was an additional contributing factor to not telling the truth. Mo was only able to gossip about me and turn the air conditioner up. Although it was certainly disagreeable, I was able to live with it. "Best to keep the lie up," I thought.

"OK, I believe you," I replied to Piri, but I had doubts about Gausika.

Despite her former romantic feelings for Mo, I decided to give her the benefit of the doubt. On Saturday morning, I messaged her to inquire if she wanted to meet up. I didn't get a reply until Sunday evening.

"Hi, Sophie. Sorry for the late reply. I forgot my phone in an Uber and only just got it back now," she replied.

This was too much.

"Sure, makes sense. It's very likely that you forgot a phone in Uber and actually would manage to get it back on Sunday," I replied.

Gausika looked furious when I saw her on Monday morning. I didn't mind because I had lost every interest in spending time with her. It was the end of our 'smoking buddy' friendship.

The humiliations and the gossip about me had become too difficult to bear. I refrained from any form of communication with my co-workers. It was quite easy as my team worked abroad. In order to block out other people's conversations about me, I listened to music the entire day. Strangely enough, I became really happy. I no longer had to pretend to be interested in dull conversations, make small talk or make-believe to be content with something when I wasn't. I still had to do my tedious, frustrating job, but I no longer had to spend time with boring and frustrating people.

Two days after I had ended the friendship with Gausika, I went for a short walk during office hours. All of a sudden, I started smiling, and I couldn't stop smiling. I started running, and I even danced on the street. It was an unfamiliar and liberating experience. A short distance from the office building, I saw Mo smoking outside by himself. How many times had I thought about him, so many times had I feared him, so many times had I worried about what other people had thought or said about me? At that moment, I was aware that none of that affected me anymore. This recognition made me feel free and happier than I ever had felt in my entire life. I realized I didn't need another human being to complete me or give me the feeling that I was something worth.

Mo was observing me without any attempt to hide it. I smiled when I passed him. It was like I was able to read his tinny mind. He was obviously very eager to know why I was suddenly so happy. The smile remained on my face the entire week. The people in the office noticed and smiled when they walked past me. The phrase "smile and the world will smile to you in return" was obviously true. Some people attempted to approach me and engage me in a conversation. I had no interest in talking to them, and therefore, I kept every conversation as short as possible. Of course, some people weren't pleased with my new found happiness at all.

"She is just happy. It has nothing to do with you. Don't be annoyed," I heard Piri say to Gausika after two weeks.

I never had the impression that Gausika wanted to see me happy. She had been resentful towards me ever since Mo had asked me to join him for a cigarette without inviting her along. Therefore, it didn't surprise me at all that my happiness annoyed her and I was even more pleased that I no longer had to spend time with her. Of course, Gausika was not the only one who was displeased with my cheerfulness. Not long after Gausika had expressed her annoyance, Amange approached Aisha.

"We need to know what is going on. We need to know why she is so happy the whole time. You need to talk to her," he said to her.

It had not been a question. It had been an order. I was somewhat amused about how desperate Amange, Mo and Brigitta were to solve the mystery of my new found lightheartedness. The commands they gave people, however, shocked me, for I simply couldn't comprehend what power they believed they had that would have enabled them to enforce their will on others. A couple of weeks later, I went for a walk around the office building. When I came back, I saw Mo standing outside with Amange.

"No, it is Sophie," he said when I walked past him.

"For fuck's sake," I thought. It was not all too difficult to guess what would happen next. Mo wanted to pursue me again as he wasn't able to accept that I was happy and he was not. I went to the toilet, and when I returned to my desk, I saw Amange sitting next to Ugne's desk. He looked exhausted, for his face was almost level with his knees. At that moment, I knew that Amange and I were thinking the same thing. "Not this shit again." I decided, however, to wait until I would react. The next day, we got an email from Ugne, which informed all employees of CooperateEvent that the seating order would change the following week. The seating order was attached to the email. "Marvellous," I thought. I saw that I would sit next to Sita, Brigatta's friend and next to Vince. Brigitta would be sitting not far from me, either. The moment of annoyance only lasted a couple of minutes. This unfortunate change of events would not take away my carefreeness. I was determined by it. On Monday, however, my resoluteness was put to the test.

"I think he wants to get back with Sophie now. This fucking wannabe," Brigitta said to Sita not long after I had taken my seat.

Sita didn't reply, and I refrained from saying something, for I didn't want to honour Brigitta's outrages remark with a response.

"Do you want to come to the event tonight?" Brigitta asked her.

"You know what? I don't think I will. I will be sitting here with Sophie."

Brigitta and Mo apparently tried to pretend again that they had broken up. "As you wish," I thought. Mo had to be stopped before his mind games would deprive me of my sleep once more. I was determined to drive Mo away with one text when I came home that evening. My observations of Mo's character during my employment at CooperateEvent made me aware of what pleased and displeased him. "I am so sorry for the things I texted you. I know it wasn't ok. It doesn't matter what I went through. I didn't have the right to insult you like this. I think I was just really upset because of my half-brother's death, and I reached out to you because of the hug you once gave me."

Mo detested any display of emotions and would certainly consider an apology a weakness. Therefore, I considered the message as cunning. The next day, I crossed Mo at the entrance to the office. He looked very upset, which only confirmed my character reading of him. I went out for a smoke. "Checkmate," I thought. Sometimes, I wondered why Mo could not look through my plan, but by the look of it, he was too much in love himself to comprehend the true purpose of the messages I had sent him. Before I left the office that day, I went into the kitchen.

"Hi, Sophie. How are you doing?" a co-worker asked.

I had never spoken to him before. He was the one who had pointed at me and said that I was the one Mo had given up everything for.

"I am good. Glad it is almost the weekend," I replied.

"I could give you a hug to make you even happier."

I suppressed a smile.

"How generous of you," I responded and walked away.

"I am asking myself what kind of IQ those people have. It's obvious that I only message Mo when he tries to chase me. Apart from that, no woman would text such things when she wants a guy," I thought. Mo was apparently not capable of comprehending that. The next day, I walked past him with a smile on my face. It only enhanced my appearance because I looked stunning that day. I was dressed in black skinny jeans and a black top. My long brown hair was wavy and falling elegantly over my shoulders. It was written on Mo's face that he found me attractive, for he suddenly looked on the ground, afraid to gaze at me too long. I went back to my desk. With a smile and satisfaction in my heart, I observed that Mo had followed. Brigitta stood up and walked past Mo, who slapped her hard on her rear end.

"Ouch," she screamed.

Afterwards, Mo starred on the breasts of a very pretty female co-worker. "Now this idiot is harassing other women as well," I thought, still smiling. I did my best to keep focusing on my work, but it was difficult to concentrate.

"Are you and Brigitta still together?" a female co-worker asked Mo.

"No, I just wanted Sophie to think we are still together."

I was very much in disbelief for what kind of idiot would say something like this within earshot of the people who were the subject of the conversation. What I couldn't understand at all was how anyone could like that moron. In fairness, now Mo could be, to a certain degree, exciting, but his stupidity was so off putting that the little pleasure he could give someone was not worth it to endure that kind of ignorance. From my desk, I observed that Brigitta packed her stuff and left the office half an hour before the end of the business day.

CHAPTER 17

To treat myself, I ordered Indian takeaway that night. Since I had discovered the taste of Indian, it always had been my preferred meal choice. With a full stomach and a relaxed mind, I lay in bed reading.

All of a sudden, the music on my iPhone started playing by itself. I trembled. I didn't know what was happening. Was my phone faulty? Did someone or something have control over it? I took the phone, restarted it and put it on my bed. I went to the other side of my room and watched it. The iTunes app opened again, and the song "Stop" by Jamelia began to play. Was it possible that Mo had hacked my phone? Or had I simply lost my mind?

The smile on my face was gone the next day. I questioned my sanity, or maybe I tried to deny the grievousness of my distressful situation. I only knew that I was no longer willing to put up with any of it. Mo and Amange were grinning when they saw me. Their smile demonstrated the power of someone in a superior position, which troubled me greatly. Hacking a phone was very much illegal, and I doubted very much that anyone from the company had the technical skills to do something like this. Nevertheless, the music had played on its own.

Unless a ghost had decided to haunt me, I had to assume that my phone had been compromised. My happiness was gone entirely. As a matter of fact, I was on the edge of tears. Before I went home that day, I bought myself a bottle of Lambrini, for it was a lot cheaper than gin and tonic.

"Is everything okay with you?" Nathalie asked me when I encountered her in the kitchen.

"All good," I replied, fully aware that I was tipsy.

In the fear of being labelled as crazy, I didn't tell anyone what I suspected. I couldn't imagine how anybody could help me and therefore saw no use in discussing the matter. My alcohol consumption increased every day, for I was no longer capable of dealing with the pain, fear and anger inside of me. "This is not life, and it's not worth it," I said to myself one evening while looking in the mirror. The reflection I saw had changed for stress, sadness, anger, and alcohol hardly increased someone's beauty.

"I will not let Mo destroy me," I said out loud.

The next day, I made my decision. I knew that I would become a shadow of myself if I stayed at CooperateEvent. Mo would never leave me alone, no matter what I did. That much was obvious.

"Hi, Iris. Can we please have a call today? I need to tell you something," I texted her.

"Sure, does four in the afternoon work for you?" she replied.

"Works fine for me," I answered.

At four, I went into a meeting room where I called Iris on Teams.

"Hi, Sophie."

"Hi, Iris."

"You said you wanted to talk to me. What is going on?"

"You know that I have a BA degree in graphic design. It became evident that I don't see my future at CooperateEvent and that I have to look for another opportunity as I wish to fulfil my creative potential."

"I get that. What exactly does that mean? Look for another opportunity. You apparently want to leave the company."

"Yes, but I want to be fair. I know you will need some time to look for a replacement for me. So, I am giving you three months' notice."

"This is very kind of you, Sophie. I wish you good luck

finding a position more suitable for your abilities. Please also give me your written notice and add Dylan to it," she replied.

"Thanks, Iris. Will do. Talk to you soon."

Although I was aware that I had to stay at the company for another three months, I felt that my mental state improved greatly, for the end of this nightmare was in sight. I had given a three months' notice to save more money as I didn't know when I would receive another offer of employment.

Nathalie had finally managed to get me into chanting. To my surprise, I felt a positive change within me. I focused on what I had to change within myself and ceased giving attention to my environment. Mo was, for some reason, absent for two entire weeks. It was like heaven. The day he came back, I met him in the kitchen. He had an evil smile on his face, which made me feel highly uncomfortable, for nothing that made Mo happy could be good news for me. I guessed that he was planning his next move. Half an hour before the end of the business day, I encountered him. He was in the company of one of his friends.

"Why? The only thing I will lose is a bet," Mo said to the co-worker.

It wasn't too difficult to guess the nature of this wager. I packed my things and left the office, doing my best to hide my anger. When I arrived at the Arnos Grove station, I took out my phone and texted Mo on Teams.

"Looks like you lost your bet. You are really pathetic. I can only feel sorry for you."

I pressed send. For me, Mo was pure evil, as I assumed that Mo's bet involved having sex with me. I was not capable of understanding the cruelty of his character. Of course, I would never have slept with Mo, but it was still hurtful and humiliating, especially when I considered that there were people in the office who had knowledge of that bet. The medicine for my emotional pain was alcohol once more. "How can anyone be this monstrous?" I thought while sitting on the ground in my room with a gin and tonic in my hand. Tears dripped down my cheeks until late in the evening.

The next day, I had my emotions back under control. I was determined that nobody would notice how hurt I really was. While I was walking to my desk, I noticed Oscar. He looked very uncomfortable at the sight of me. I was, therefore, certain that Mo had told everyone about the bet and the text I had sent him the previous evening. Amange arrived at the office only a couple of minutes after me.

"Who told Sophie?" he asked a co-worker.

That question was proof that my suspicion had been accurate. The bet had involved me. I went into the kitchen to make myself a cup of coffee. My determination made me act like a victorious warrior who had just won a battle. I smiled to hide my pain and anger. In the kitchen, I met Mo. He was in the presence of clients. His face was distorted with rage. It was a look that was impossible to forget. He considered the revelation of my knowledge of his bet an insult. There was no sign of remorse and no sign of shame. Mo evidently could not see anything wrong with his character and actions. I smiled at him defensively to make him believe that none of that affected me. I returned to my desk beaming.

"She thinks she won," Amange said without troubling to keep his voice down.

"She did win," another co-worker replied.

I looked up and caught sight of Mo. He showed the middle finger to a co-worker, and his face was distorted with rage. The look on his face and his outrageous behaviour made him very ugly indeed. I was beyond shocked as he had done it in the presence of Dylan and the clients. "Why on earth does Dylan not tell Mo that this behaviour is unacceptable? What must the clients think, and why is Dylan not concerned that Mo's inappropriate conduct will reflect badly on the entire company?" I thought. At lunch, I encountered Amange outside. He was looking in my direction. In response, I smiled. For them, it was a game, and I didn't want to give them the satisfaction that they were able to hurt me. Two hours later, I went out for a smoke again. Mo walked out of the office building with his backpack over his right shoulder when I lighted my cigarette. He didn't look at me and walked straight in the direction of the train station. I was watching him defensively. At the pedestrian crossing, he turned his face in my direction. It was hard to guess what went through his mind at that moment, but I hoped that Mo had bet a good deal of money. His loss was my gain.

The day had been hell, and I was relieved when it was over. When I arrived at the Arnos Grove station, the iTunes app opened, and the song "Steppin' to the bad side" started playing on its own. I was, therefore, one hundred per cent certain that Mo had access to my phone. "I can't anymore," I thought when I was back in my room. Every day was terror and torture. I was emotionally and physically completely exhausted. "Why can't he just leave me alone? This is insane," I thought. The next day, I wasn't able to smile anymore, and the people from the office noticed.

"It is absolutely horrible," I heard a girl say.

"Yes, but when you are so discriminated like that," Vince replied.

"Do they really think that they have a right to do something like this just because I texted Mo that he is a stupid Muslim?" I thought. I tried to focus on work, but it was nearly impossible. "This piece of shit tried to seduce me, although he was in a relationship with Brigitta the day he and I kissed. Yes. I have expressed my anger in a rude way. That does not make me a racist, and it's certainly not an excuse for this constant harassment," I said inside my head.

Later, I went out for a smoke, where I met a new starter who was very nice. Mo and Amange were outside as well. I tried to have a conversation with the new starter but was distracted when Amange said to Mo, 'We simply follow her. When she is doing something that she shouldn't do, then we have her.' This was psycho terror, and it was proof that they had access to my phone. How else would they have been able to follow me? Later in the day, I saw Mo going out with Brigitta. When she came back, she was looking at me. I observed her for a brief moment, but her facial expression was hard to read.

"He told me that he only ditched me because Sophie is that nice-looking, but he said that it is not really worth it," she told a couple of her friends.

"If they buy that crap, then they are really stupid," I thought, for I was certain that Brigitta had known about the bet, and their breakup had been nothing else but pretence. "If Mo really would have ditched Brigitta, then she would have been sad the next day, but she was not sad at all. And if Mo really would have broken up with her, then she would never have talked about it within my earshot. Why do people not see how evil Brigitta and Mo really are?" I asked myself.

I distracted myself with music, and it worked for a short

duration.

"She wants me to meet her in the middle now," Mo said while I was listening to the song 'The middle' by Zedd.

"How the hell is Mo able to know what kind of music I am listening to?" I thought. "And how is this asshole able to think that I still like him? Is he delusional? I mean, he made a bet that probably involved having sex with me. Now, he tells everyone in the office that I want him to meet me in the middle. He is fucking insane."

My body couldn't deal with the constant stress and psycho-terror anymore. I began to feel ill. Every day, I had painful muscle tension and a headache. I knew that my body and my mind wouldn't be able to endure another month of torture. On Friday, late in the afternoon, I went out for a smoke, where I met Owen.

"Hi, Sophie. How are you doing?" he asked.

"I have been diagnosed with cancer. The doctor told me that I would have three to four months to live," I said.

"Oh, my god. Are you serious?"

"Yes, it's the first time I have told anyone."

"I don't know what to say. I am so sorry."

"Yes, I can't really believe it myself yet," I said while trying to look as sad as possible.

"If you need someone to talk to, I will be there."

"That's very kind of you, but I just want to be alone."

"I understand that. Let me know if there is anything I can do for you."

"Thanks, I appreciate that," I responded.

I went back upstairs. Naturally, by the end of the day, the news about my terminal illness had been spread around in the office. After another cigarette break, I met Mo in front of the elevator. He looked upset. I wondered if that man was able to feel compassion for someone. At five, I took my laptop with me, determined never to return to that office. I didn't feel guilty because I had told another lie, for I had done it to save my life. "They should feel guilty for doing this to me," I thought. The next day, I went to Starbucks to celebrate my new freedom.

"That's five pounds fifty, please," the barista said.

I took the headphones out of my ears and paused the music to be able to hear what she was saying. At that moment, the Notes app opened. Typed in was "I put so much effort in p." Incredulous, I starred at the message.

"This has gone through. Thanks," the barista said.

I didn't reply. "This is fucking sick," I thought. Mo was typing into my phone, although he believed that I had cancer. In other words, that man was stressing out a dying person. "He is an insane monster," I thought. When I got home, I called Apple customer service. I explained the situation and described that the music had played on its own on several occasions and that things had been typed in.

"Did anyone have access to your phone or iCloud email," he asked.

"It's possible. Yes," I replied.

"OK, let me check a couple of things."

Ten minutes later, he informed me that he couldn't find anything.

"I suggest you reset your phone to factory settings and change your iCloud email and password just to be safe," he concluded.

"Is that all? What if someone has hacked my phone?" I asked.

"It's impossible to hack an iPhone. I can assure you that."

"OK, thanks," I replied and hung up.

I was annoyed, for I was certain that Mo had access to my phone, and I would have loved to prove it. "This piece of shit should go to jail," I thought furiously. In the process of resetting my phone to factory settings, I was asked for the password I used on my other phone. I thought it was highly suspicious, for I only possessed one iPhone. "Apple should be able to deal with that," I figured. Later in the day, Nathalie and I went for a walk in Hampstead. Nathalie had asked me to come along with her to dog-sitting a beautiful puppy and thought that I would enjoy the exercise. On the way, I informed her that I would be working from home until the last day of employment due to the stress Mo had caused me. She seemed to understand and thought it was a good idea. The park in Hampstead was really beautiful, and the weather was ideal for a nice long walk. I felt more relaxed than I had in weeks.

"No, I can't go back now because I don't have time," I heard someone shout.

Nathalie and I looked around to see who was screaming, but nobody was close to us. It was most mysterious.

"Look what you did to Sophie. Fucking evil," the girl said.

"Sounds bad. Should we go back and check what is going on?" Nathalie asked.

"No, let's keep walking," I replied.

The voice we had heard sounded very much like Brigitta's, and as she had mentioned my name, I was certain it had been her.

CHAPTER 18

I hadn't told Iris that I was working from home, for I was aware that she would disapprove. Mo and his friends were destroying me; therefore, working remotely was the only option if I wanted to survive. It was a lot easier to fulfil my job duties at home as I was finally able to concentrate. I was, of course, aware that Mo had still somehow access to my phone, but I no longer had to listen to people's gossip about me. On Thursday, I stepped outside the house to smoke at about seven in the evening. I looked out on the street and saw Mo and Brigitta drive by in a black BMW X5. "Are they now stalking me at my home?" I asked myself. My body froze, and I felt my muscles contract. "This is just sick. Why are they doing this? What is the point?" I asked myself. "Does nobody see how insane this is? How cruel they are," I thought. I was mentally completely exhausted. They drove by my house almost every evening from then on. It was a devastating experience which caused me anxiety, discomfort and stress.

As I was stalked on a daily basis, the people at CooperateEvent were most certainly aware that I had been lying about my terminal illness. I didn't care whether they were judging me or not, for my opinion of them was very ill indeed. They had supported Mo and Brigitta, although their actions and intentions could only be described as evil. In my eyes, the people who didn't stand up to a crime of that nature were not much better than the villain itself.

On the second last day of employment, I had a call with my team to say goodbye. They all wished me the best for my future, and we parted on good terms. On the last day, I was obliged to return my laptop and have an exit interview with Tina, the new HR woman. I walked towards her desk while doing my best to ignore the people who were watching me, but I found the experience devastating, for I was certain that everyone knew that Mo had access to my phone. The humiliation was almost unbearable.

"Hi, Sophie."

"Hi, Tina."

"Please give your laptop to Vince and then meet me in the meeting room number three."

Vince was not in the office, and neither was Brigitta or

Mo. Therefore, I just left the laptop on Vince's desk. On the way to the meeting room, I experienced backflashes of all the unpleasant memories.

"How are you doing?" Tina asked when I had entered the room.

"I am fine."

"Great, I need to ask you a couple of questions. It's standard procedure,"

"No problem."

All of her questions inquired about how I perceived the company.

"Why did you decide to leave CooperateEvent?" she asked after about five minutes of interrogation.

"I am a graphic designer. I want to pursue a more creative career path. Therefore, I decided to work freelance as a designer."

"I understand that. Was there any personal reason why you decided to leave the company?" she asked.

"Yes, one reason was Mo. He and I once kissed. Afterwards, I rejected him. Then he was shouting in the office that he wanted to destroy my life. It was real terror."

"I see. But you know that Mo has left the company?" she replied without any concern on her face.

"Did he now?"

"Yes, he left two weeks ago."

I didn't reply.

"Well, that is it. Thank you so much for all your hard work. I wish you all the best for your future."

"Thanks, Tina. I wish you all the best, too."

I took my bag and left. Tina had reminded me why I had never told anyone the truth. She didn't even ask why I never had reported Mo. An attitude like that was why I was scared to speak up.

"How was your last day?" Nathalie asked me when I arrived at home.

"It was fine. I am glad it is over."

"Oh, good. I am so happy for you. Maybe you want to do some chanting with me later."

"Not today. I will get myself a pizza and some drinks. Then I will watch a movie. Maybe tomorrow."

"Sure, no problem," she replied.

I felt relieved. "This nightmare is finally over," I thought. The next day, it became apparent that I had thought wrong. Mo and Brigitta kept driving by my house every evening for one week. It was insane. I googled Mo and found out that he had left CooperateEvent because he had joined a start-up design agency located in Finsbury Park. This discovery was mental torture, for working for a design agency had always been my dream, but the revelation pushed me to work harder to find a designer job myself. After one month, I finally got my first freelance job as a graphic designer, which was located in Waterford. I had to wake up every morning at five o'clock, which was exhausting. I didn't mind, for I hoped it would be my breakthrough. After a couple of days, I got accustomed to it, and the work was rewarding. I had to create animations with the content they provided. It was still not a dream job, but it was certainly a start.

"She got all obsessed with Mo," I heard a guy in the office say on my fifth day. Fear paralyzed me. Had it been a coincidence? Had he been talking about me? "It's very unlikely that he knows Mo. They must be talking about someone else," I thought. However, I got the gut feeling again. Mo had said after I had rejected him that he wanted to destroy my life. "But how can he make stuff about me public," I thought. I thought it best to keep focusing on my job and not jump to conclusions. After two weeks, I got a call from the head-hunter. She informed me that the company didn't have enough work for me before Christmas but that it was likely that my services would be required again after the holidays.

On the twentieth of December, I flew to Switzerland to spend Christmas with my sister. The journey was not enjoyable because I worried about money and Mo's creepy stalking. As a matter of fact, I was on the edge of tears by the time I landed at the Zurich airport. I was aware that I would have to meet my father as well. It gave me additional discomfort, for my father never had made me feel good about myself. After my mother's death, he had criticized me every day. It had been a horrible experience.

I met my sister at the Zurich train station at six in the evening under the big clock. At the sight of her, I managed to smile despite my anxious mind.

"Hi, Sophie."

I gave her a hug.

"Hi, Piera."

"How was the journey?" she asked without looking too happy.

"All did go well," I replied.

"Good, have you eaten anything?"

"I had a sandwich, but that was hours ago."

"Are you hungry now, or can you wait until we are at my place?"

"I could eat now."

"I know a good Chinese in the train station."

"Great," I replied.

She walked on, and I followed her in silence.

"What do you want?" she asked with a grim face.

"I take the beef noodles," I replied.

She ordered for both of us. I took out my card.

"I will pay. You don't have any money," she said,

emphasizing the last two words.

"OK, thanks," I replied while feeling lesser of a person because she had money and I didn't.

We ate our food without having a conversation at all. On the journey to her place, we hardly talked either.

"You have no data. I will connect you to my hotspot. Give me your phone," she said and took the phone out of my hand without waiting for my response while we were sitting in the tram.

I was uncomfortable with this, but I didn't dare say anything. My sister's apartment was beautiful, very modern and stylishly decorated. She had a really big living room and a beautiful kitchen. I couldn't help but feel a bit sad and jealous because I was living in a shared house, and she was living like this. She showed me where I would be sleeping. It was a small bed in her home office.

"I have to call a friend of mine now. She needs my advice as a lawyer," she said.

"No problem," I replied while wondering why she was keen to talk to her friend and not to me.

I felt awkward sitting there without having anything to do while my sister was on the phone for one hour. In order to distract myself, I smoked more than I should have done.

"Right, I have to wake up early tomorrow as I still have to do some work. Therefore, I go to bed now," she said.

"It's Saturday tomorrow."

"I know that, but we have a really big case. Lawyers need to work sometimes at the weekend as well. I will give you the spare key so that you can go out. You can also watch TV if you prefer."

"OK, thanks," I replied.

I asked myself if I was too sensitive or if my sister wasn't happy to have me around. Exhausted and sad, I went to bed. The next day, I woke up feeling uneasy, for I didn't feel my presence was welcome in my sister's apartment.

"Good morning. Did you sleep alright?" Piera asked me while looking again annoyed.

"Yes, thanks."

"Good, I have to do my yoga now."

I made myself a cup of coffee, which I took out with me on the balcony. While smoking a cigarette, I thought my sister had it all. She had a successful career, a husband and friends. The only thing I had to show for after all this hard work at college was a creepy stalker. In comparison, I considered myself a failure. After Piera had finished her exercise, she showered and dressed.

"Right, I will come home at about six," she said.

"OK, have a good day," I said downheartedly.

"Thanks," she replied.

Once she had left, tears poured down my cheeks. It took

me a while to calm myself, for everything felt overwhelming. In the afternoon, I went to the closest shop to buy groceries, for I had decided to make a beautiful dinner for me and my sister. "Maybe she is just stressed because she has so much work to do. I will cook for her so she doesn't have to do it herself when she gets home," I thought. I bought steaks, asparagus and potatoes. It was way more expensive in Switzerland than it was in England. I wasn't sure if it was wise to spend that much money, but then I dismissed my objections, for I had a freelance job waiting for me after Christmas. The rest of the afternoon, I watched Christmas movies, and at five, I started cooking.

"Hi," I said to Piera when she arrived home at quarter past six.

She looked annoyed and didn't reply.

"Is everything okay?" I asked.

"Yes, you made a bit of a mess," she hissed.

I felt tears coming into my eyes but suppressed them.

"I will clean up afterwards," I said.

"Don't mind. I will do it," she replied, clearly annoyed.

She went into her room, and I did my best to bring my emotions back under control.

"Piera, dinner is ready," I said ten minutes later.

"Yes, I am coming," she replied in an unpleasant tone.

We sat at the dining table and began to eat.

"It's really good," she said.

"Thanks," I replied, slightly happier, for she had finally said something nice.

"How much did it cost you?" she asked.

"About forty Swiss Francs," I replied.

"Right, I will give you the money tomorrow. You quit your job, so I have to pay for you," she said.

"Only if you want to. I am working freelance as a designer and can afford to pay for a meal," I replied, feeling like she had only offered me the money because she had felt obliged to.

After we had finished our dinner, she cleaned the dishes.

"Do you need help with that?" I asked politely.

"No, I will do it myself," she snapped.

I went out for a cigarette. "What did I do wrong?" I thought. Afterwards, we watched a Christmas movie but hardly spoke a word.

"I am tired. I think I want to go to bed," I said at half past ten.

"What? It's not even twelve yet."

"I know. But I am tired."

"OK, goodnight."

My downheartedness prevented me from falling asleep easily. "Am I a horrible person? Do I deserve this treatment?" I thought. The next morning, we ate breakfast together.

"Do you want to go to Starbucks later?" she asked.

"Yes, I would like that," I replied.

We took the tram to town an hour later. In the coffee shop, she paid again, but it became apparent that she only did it because she felt bound to. When we had sat down, Piera took a newspaper from the table and read it. She didn't talk to me at all. I observed that other customers were giving us curious looks. It was so humiliating.

"Our father will come at six tonight. I will do the cooking," she said.

"OK," I replied, fully aware that my displeasure was audible in my voice.

"I hope it won't be awkward between the two of you," she retorted.

My response to this comment was silence, for any remark on my side would have resulted in a fight. My father arrived, unfortunately punctually. I hadn't expected it because he was usually always late in my childhood. My sister appeared to be excited to see him. When he walked through the door, I went reluctantly to greet him. After that awkward welcome, we sat down at the dining table, and my sister brought us drinks with happiness written on her face.

"So, how is it going with your freelance job?" my father asked.

"It's going well. They will have some work for me after Christmas," I replied as confident as possible.

"Ah," he replied with doubt in his voice.

"What exactly do you have to do in your job?" my sister asked.

"I have to create animations with content they give me. It's pretty cool," I replied politely despite my annoyance that my sister hadn't asked me that question before.

"Oh, great. Can we see it somewhere?" she said.

I took out my phone and showed them what I had done for the company on Instagram.

"Very nice," she said, high-pitched.

"It's astonishing what you can do with smartphones these days. Like tracking the location of a person," my father said.

I failed to comprehend why my father would say something like this. It was probably a weird coincidence, but it was suspicious when I considered that I was stalked by a psycho and his pathetic girlfriend. I decided to ignore his inappropriate remark, for I didn't wish to fight that early in the evening. During dinner, I told them that I practised Buddhism and meditated to lead the conversation in a favourable direction.

"I feel a positive change within me when I try to focus my mind and manifest what I desire," I said.

"Oh, amazing. Did you ever read the book 'Siddhartha' by

Herman Hesse?" my father asked.

"No, I haven't read it yet, but I think I would like to," I replied.

"I think I still have a copy. I will send it to you," my father said enthusiastically.

Naturally, this conversation had pleased my father, for he always had liked to make himself important by talking about the things he knew. He had always appeared pompous to me. That, in combination with the ill-treatment I had received from him, made it simply impossible for me to like him. The rest of the evening went well, although my father talked a lot about my other sister, who had stopped talking to him after my mother's death. What he said about her wasn't nice, but I thought it was best not to express my opinion. At the end of the evening, I gave my father a hug to say goodbye.

"You did well," Piera told me after he had taken his leave.

We parted on good terms, for my sister's behaviour towards me had improved after my father had given her the impression that he had approved of me.

CHAPTER 19

"Welcome back," Nathalie said when I arrived home on December twenty-seventh.

"Thanks, how was your Christmas?" I asked.

"It was really good. How was yours?"

"Really good. I spend it with my sister and father," I replied, for the truth would have been way too complicated to explain.

"Oh, it's so nice that you could spend the holidays with your family."

I smiled to make her believe that spending Christmas with my father and my sister had been nice. She went off and came back a minute later with a present in her hand.

"This is for you," she said cheerfully.

"Oh, this is so nice. Thanks," I said, taken very much by surprise.

I opened it eagerly because my family hadn't given me any presents. My sister had said that she had to pay for me in the restaurant and Starbucks and that this had been my present. Nathalie had given me incense sticks and a candle. It was only something small, but it made me happy.

"It's for your meditation and chanting," she said.

"It's perfect. I feel bad now because I don't have anything for you," I replied.

"Don't be silly. It's just something really small," she said.

"Well, thanks again," I replied.

Josh had been watching us the whole time. Maybe it was imagination, but he had looked jealous. "Why should he be?" I thought. The next day, I went to town to buy a little present for Nathalie.

"You shouldn't have," she said when I gave it to her.

"I know. I just wanted to," I replied.

On the twenty-eight of December, I got a call from the head-hunter. The freelance job had been cancelled as they apparently didn't have enough work. I found myself in a really awful predicament because I didn't have enough money to pay the rent and other bills. First, I called my sister Piera and asked her for financial support. She said that she couldn't help me, for she soon had to pay taxes. Then I called my other sister because she was the only one who hadn't spent her inheritance money yet. She said she wouldn't help and that I shouldn't have quit my job. She also told me that I was thirty years old and I didn't have my life under control. I tried to explain to her that I had resigned because of a guy that was stalking me.

"You and your stupid problems the whole time," she said and hung up the phone.

I was on the verge of tears, but then I took a deep breath and called my father, fully aware that nothing he would say would do me any good.

"Well, it was your fault because you did quit your job," he said.

"I need to borrow money."

"Now you want money from me?"

I trembled with fear and anger.

"From me, you are not getting any more money. All the horrible things you said to me during your life. How many times did you yell at me?"

"You told me as a child that you have to be mean to me because the world will be mean to me, too. You were hitting me in front of a school friend. You told my mother that it is ok to hit a child. You put me down in front of other people and made me believe that I wasn't worth anything," I replied.

My voice was shaking.

"You don't talk to me this way," he yelled and hung up the phone.

Fear, shock and emotional pain made it impossible to think clearly in that moment. After fifteen minutes of trying to calm myself, I walked to the closest shop and bought a bottle of gin and two packs of painkillers. I texted my family that I would commit suicide. After I had sent the messages, I smashed my phone against the wall. The phone was broken, not unlike myself. I swallowed the two packs of painkillers with water. In order to give the painkillers an extra kick, I made myself a gin and tonic and went outside. "Why is my family treating me like this, and why have they always been so mean to me my entire life?" I asked myself while smoking a cigarette. After one hour, I felt the effects of the painkillers and the alcohol. I went to bed and hoped that I would die, for the pain and fear were not to be endured.

The next day, I woke up early, regretting my anger outburst from the previous evening. "I can't believe I smashed my phone last night," I thought. I wasn't happy that I was still alive, for living was pain, and living my life was fear, but the suicide attempt had failed and maybe for a good reason. I went to central London to buy a new iPhone, but I was so weak from the painkiller overdose that I was hardly able to walk. I had to extend my contract with Three for another two years, but I knew that if I still wanted to live, I needed a phone. In the store, I put the sim card from the old phone into the new iPhone. I got a text from my sister Piera immediately after the set up was complete.

"Sophie, are you still alive? Can you answer please?" she had asked.

Instead of replying, I went to Southbank and asked myself if I should jump into the river. Was I such a monster that I deserved to be treated like this by people? "I don't really want to give up, but I also don't know how I can stay alive when the only thing I get from humans is hate," I thought. Something was holding me back. A part of me believed that I still could make something out of my life. At eight in the evening, I was aware that I didn't really want to die. Therefore, I returned home.

"Is everything okay with you, Sophie?" Nathalie asked me once I had entered the living room.

I informed her that the freelance job had been cancelled and that my father didn't want to help me, although he had about three hundred thousand in his bank account.

"Your father needs to help you. It's his duty," she replied.

"Yeah, he should," I replied while feeling even more terrible as Nathalie had confirmed that my father's behaviour towards me was no ok at all.

I texted my sister back in my room to inform her that I was still alive. Afterwards, I called my father and informed him that I had tried to kill myself and that without his financial support, I wouldn't be able to pay my bills.

"OK, I will lend you the money, but you are blackmailing me."

"Thanks. Please ensure that you will transfer it within three days. Otherwise, I won't be able to pay the rent, and I will be homeless."

"Again, you are blackmailing me. I said I will give you the money," he hissed.

"Thanks. I will give you the money back once I have a new job," I replied and hung up the phone.

"How is that blackmailing? I was only asking for help," I thought. My suicidal thoughts didn't vanish after the call. Quite the opposite. The money was just one problem. Mo and Brigitta were stalking me, and my family was rude and cold towards me. In other words, I was alone. Lost in my dark thoughts, I walked to the shop and bought again a bottle of Lambrini and painkillers. I took some of the painkillers, but not all of them. At about ten, I called my father.

"I am suicidal."

He didn't say anything for about two minutes.

"Hello," I said.

"Sophie, I am not well. I can't talk now," he replied and hung up.

I was numb. What kind of person would give such a response to the declaration of suicide thoughts? I went out for a smoke. Mo and Brigitta were standing in front of the gate.

"She is okay," Brigitta said, then she and Mo left.

I was in no condition to go after them. It was too overwhelming for me. I just stood there paralyzed and smoked. Back inside my room, I took the rest of the painkillers and finished the bottle of Lambrini. "I don't know. Maybe I deserve to be treated like this by humans. Maybe I am something monstrous. I must be. Otherwise, people wouldn't do those things to me," I thought again.

"I just want to die," I said quietly while I was lying in bed.

It was insane that I thought that I deserved this. A part of me was aware of it, but it was hard to believe that this kind of treatment was unjustified when even your own family treats you that belittling. The next day, I decided to go to the hospital and get help. When I told the nurse in charge that I had taken a painkiller overdose in order to take my life, I was immediately led into a different room.

"We will have to do some blood tests, and then someone will come and talk to you," she said.

I waited a long time with someone in the room watching me while I was lost in my dark and gloomy thoughts. In the evening, a psychiatrist came to see me. When I told her what happened, she looked shocked.

"You went through a lot. You will need help. We will contact the Home Treatment team at once. You have to stay here tonight. We need to keep you under observation because of the painkillers you took," she said.

They gave me a bed and placed someone in the room who was watching me. The next day, the psychiatrist attended to me in the company of a doctor. The doctor told me that the blood tests were good.

"If we would send you home, do you think you would try it again?" the psychiatrist asked.

"I think I will be ok," I replied.

They discharged me and told me that someone from the Home Treatment team would soon be in touch to arrange a visit.

"Sophie, come here, please, for a second," Nathalie said when I was about to enter my room.

Reluctantly, I walked towards her, determined to keep any conversation with her short.

"Where have you been?" she demanded while looking up and down at me.

"I was out."

"Have you been in the hospital?"

"I don't want to talk about it," I replied while feeling mortified.

"I need to know what is going on. What if anything happens to you? Who would I call?"

"I can give you my sister's number later."

Without waiting for her response, I went into my room and began to apply for some jobs. Later in the evening, I heard Josh talking to Nathalie through the walls of my room.

"I don't want Sophie in this house. You need to kick her out."

This was just too much. "Doesn't he realize that I can hear him? Why does nobody think that my feelings matter?" I thought. I went again to the hospital because I was about to cut my wrist. "Nobody would be able to handle that much pain and fear," I said to myself. When I came back, I saw that Nathalie had company. I went into my room without saying anything to them.

"I can't believe that they have contacted you," her friend told her.

"I have never seen anyone as hated as Sophie," another friend remarked.

"Let's help her," one of the women said.

"I don't want to," Nathalie replied.

I didn't want to go to the hospital again, so I called the suicide hotline. I told the woman on the phone about my father's abusive behaviour in my childhood, that I had been bullied in school, that my mother had died when I was twenty-three years old and recounted the entire story with Mo. The worst part was that I saw Mo and Brigitta driving by my house while I was talking about my disturbing and painful life experiences.

"You did the right thing to reject that guy. He sounds like a very bad man to me," the woman from the hotline remarked.

CHAPTER 20

I didn't know how I had managed to get some sleep that night, but I did. The next morning, I made myself a cup of coffee and then went out for a smoke, torn between wanting to live and wanting to die. When I returned to my room, I received an email from Adecco. The content of that email informed me that my application had been forwarded to the second-largest Supermarket chain in the United Kingdom and that the company had been really impressed with my application. A zoom interview was scheduled for the following day. "Oh, my god. I can't believe it," I thought cheerfully. I replied immediately to inform them how delighted I was. Shortly afterwards, I received a call from the Home Treatment team. They announced their visit in about ten minutes. Nathalie was not at home, but Josh was. When the Home Treatment team arrived, I led them into my room. We talked about the suicide attempt, the story with Mo and the situation with my family. I told them as well about the conversations I had overhead in the house. It was humiliating and painful to share these experiences with total strangers. They had a very concerned look on their face, but it was obvious that they had no idea how I felt.

"It's a lot to deal with. Take one step at a time and be good to yourself," the man said.

I didn't find his advice very useful, for they obviously weren't able to understand how overwhelming the situation was. Once they had left, I went out for a smoke. On the way outside, I encountered Josh. He appeared to be in distress. Back in my room, I began my interview preparation. The occupation felt liberating, for it distracted me from my sorrows. Nathalie came home three hours later.

"She tried to kill herself," I heard Josh say to her.

"Ach," Nathalie replied.

Nathalie and I had been chanting and had watched movies together several times. Therefore, I wasn't able to comprehend the complete lack of empathy and concern in her tone. Later in the day, my father sent me the Western Union receipt. He had transferred me one thousand pounds. It was enough to pay the rent and to get by for another month. I had to go to Central London to collect the money. On the journey home, I considered my situation. "Is the behaviour of my family normal?" I asked myself. I concluded that it wasn't. The people I had spoken to had been outraged about the way my family was treating me. They had made clear that my father had been abusive and that he most likely suffered from a narcissistic personality disorder. He had devalued me, hit me and manipulated people not to like me. He also made other people, like my mother and my sister, believe that abusive behaviour was acceptable.

I recalled that my family and I once had been in a restaurant to celebrate my father's birthday. Suddenly, out of the blue, he had said, 'We are well dressed, except Sophie.' My father had belittled me in front of everyone at the birthday party. I remembered the day a school friend had visited me and that my father had hit me hard in the face in front of her. The worst memory of my father was, however, when he told me that he had to be mean to me because everyone would be mean to me. It's something that I never had been able to forget. It came to my mind that I once had told my uncle Rolf and my aunt Susanne about the way my father had behaved towards me. My sister Piera had been present when I spoke out about the ill-treatment. The next day, my father approached me to disclose that Piera had made him aware that I had told my uncle and aunt about his behaviour towards me. He said that he would sue me if I ever told anyone again. When I had asked my sister why she had told my father, she had just replied, 'This is my father you are talking about.'

I had made my decision by the end of the day. In an email, I informed my father that I never wished to talk to him again because of the things he had done to me in my childhood and because he had hung up the phone when I had informed him about my suicide thoughts. I ceased the contact with my sister Piera as well. She had protected my father because she had wanted his approval, although she had known that he had been abusive towards me. I was torn afterwards between relief and grief. No contact meant that my family would not get another chance to hurt me, but it also meant that I was alone in this world.

The next morning, I woke up early feeling excited about my interview. I went out for a smoke and took my phone with me to listen to some music. Suddenly, the iMessage app opened. In an existing chat was typed in the word 'Scap.' I had no idea what it meant and thought I would deal with it after the interview. "I can't believe that I have answered their questions this competently despite the horror situation I find myself in," I thought after the meeting. "I have a good feeling about it, but I can't be sure. I have to wait and see," I thought. After the interview, I googled the word 'Scap.' A little while later, I found a website called Urban dictionary. The word 'Scap' meant 'A person that is messed up or annoying like a sibling or society itself.'

I had enough. Mo had apparently found a way to get access to my new phone again despite my several attempts to prevent him from doing so. "I will kill him. He won't get away with this. I have been putting up with this sick psycho for way too long," I thought. The plan was to go the following day to Finsbury Park, where Mo's office was and bide my time until he would show himself. The plan wasn't well thought through. I was well aware of it, but I thought it wouldn't matter anyway because I didn't have anything left to lose.

The next day, I woke up early, went into the kitchen, made myself a cup of coffee and chose a sharp knife as a murder weapon. The consequences would be severe if I would succeed in taking Mo's life. I was not in ignorance of it, but the prospect of endless mental torture from him appeared to be worse to me that day than a prison sentence. Although Mo certainly would not finish work until five in the evening, I took the bus early in the morning. It was more an impulsive decision rather than a rational one. When I arrived in Finsbury Park, it was half past nine. I walked to his office to investigate if the place held a good hiding spot to bide my time until the opportunity to attack would present itself.

"I don't understand what she is doing here when she is not here to see you," I heard someone say when I walked past his office.

I looked around, but nobody was close to me. It was most bizarre. In order to pass the time, I went for a walk in the park. The weather, however, was not suitable to spend the entire day outside. Therefore, I went into the pub after one hour. I assumed that alcohol would provide me with the necessary courage to kill Mo. I took my drink outside with me and lighted a cigarette. After ten minutes, Mo appeared on the scene. He had taken the sleeping bag of a homeless person and had placed himself under a bridge. He looked at me from a far distance. A woman approached him.

"What are you doing?" she asked.

"I just want Sophie to think that I am homeless now," Mo replied.

"This fucking idiot. How can anyone like this man?" I thought. I was in disbelief. "He is so stupid that he isn't event worth the crime," I figured. At that moment, I decided that I wouldn't take Mo's life no matter what he had done to me or still was doing to me. "He is just a pathetic guy who can't handle a rejection," I reckoned. I went back home, but the anger didn't vanish. Mo's appearance below the bridge had not been a coincidence. Quite the opposite. It provided additional evidence that he was able to access my location whenever he wanted. I decided to keep my options open.

Literally, two minutes after arriving home, I received a call from Adecco. The woman I spoke to informed me that the company I had interviewed for wanted to offer me the position as a freelance graphic designer.

"Oh, my god. Really? This is great. For me, this is a dream coming true," I said.

"You deserved it. They were very impressed with your skills and answers to their questions. Congratulations," she said.

I could hardly believe it. I would work for a well-known brand. Me. The girl that a psycho stalked, the girl that had such a traumatic childhood. The success filled me with pride, for I had accomplished to acquire a dream job, although I found myself in an impossible situation. At that moment, I became aware of how glad I was that I hadn't succeeded in taking my own or Mo's life. "Any form of abuse causes the victim severe emotional pain, but the abuser was and never will be worth it to end a life," I figured. I learned that day that no matter how difficult and painful life can be, happiness and success will always return when you least expect it. Of course, I had to remind myself of it sometimes.

Mo still had access to my phone, but I knew this was not the right time to do anything about it. All he could do was type silly words into my iPhone and control the music apps, and I could live with that.

On the morning of my first day of employment, I woke up

feeling highly enthusiastic, for I felt like I was finally winning in life. After all the bad things that happened to me, I would be working as a graphic designer for one of the biggest brands in the United Kingdom. If that wasn't cause for celebration, I didn't know what was. Once I had entered the office, I noticed how stylish it was. I was not used to that, for CooperateEvent didn't even have decorations on the walls. The manager greeted me in a friendly way, and I immediately felt great about this job. I was shown around in the office, introduced to people, given my MacBook and made acquainted with the working process. It had been better than I ever could have hoped for. I was in such a good mood by the time I came home for the work I would conduct in my new job would be very creative and fulfilling indeed. I hadn't smiled that much since; well, I couldn't remember for how long. In the kitchen, I encountered Nathalie. She asked me how my first day had been.

"I absolutely love it," I said with a huge smile and confidence in my tone of voice.

"I am so happy for you," she replied.

I made myself a healthy, delicious dinner that evening, which I ate in my room. At about eight, I went into the bathroom. I brought my phone with me to be able to listen to music while taking a shower. Just when I came out, I heard Josh talking to Nathalie.

"My god, this is mad. Now I finally see why Sophie has been so stressed the whole time," Josh said.

"Let's not tell her," Nathalie replied.

I walked past the living room and saw that Josh was looking at his laptop with a shocked look on his face. Josh's remark demanded that I insist they show me what was so mad, but I was too afraid. I just started a new job and was aware that I could lose it if I would deal with it instead of focusing on my work. Additionally, I was afraid of what I would see, for it certainly could be nothing good. The next morning, I looked for my wallet but couldn't find it. It was a nightmare. I called the bank straight away. The woman from the customer service hotline informed me that my card would be cancelled immediately and that I would be able to get cash at the branch. The iMessage app opened on its own after I had ended the call. In an existing chat, it had been typed "Voo to pop I Mo chill." I took a screenshot of it but was aware that I couldn't do anything about it at that moment. As I didn't have any cash at home, I had to sneak into the tube behind someone who had paid. "I can't believe this. How can anyone be that unlucky," I thought.

"That's very unfortunate to lose your wallet after your first day in a new job," my manager responded after I had explained the situation to him.

He completely understood and had no objections when I

requested to finish half an hour early to be able to get cash at the bank. Although it was difficult to concentrate on everything that was going on, I still managed to perform well. At half past four, I left the office and went to the bank. When I told the cashier I needed to withdraw money, he asked me why I didn't use the cash machine. I explained the situation to him. He turned to his college.

"Ah, Wasaibei. She probably was wasted and lost her wallet because of that."

Wasaibei was Mo's last name. I was in shock. Why did this guy know Mo, and more importantly, why did he know me? Without giving him a response, I took the cash and left the bank. My head was spinning. Somehow, I managed to keep it together despite my confusion, fear and anger. I bought an Oyster card and then took the bus. I had been so distracted that I had taken the wrong one. When I waited for the right bus, I took out my phone. The Notes app opened again by itself. Typed in was the word liar. "This fucking psycho," I thought. I took a screenshot of it. On the journey home, I combined the screenshot with an image of Mo, which I found online. With a photo editing app, I wrote 'The Joker' on top of it. I painted his eyes dark and his lips red to make Mo look like the joker from the movie 'The Dark Knight.' Out of the blue, I heard Mo's voice.

"Sophie is making fun of me," he said.

Was I going crazy? Was the stress causing a psychotic episode? "How on earth am I able to hear Mo's voice inside my head?" I did well the next day at work until I heard someone say, 'She took a screenshot of it and then combined it with an image of Mo. She knows now.' I was frozen on my desk.

"I doubt that she still likes him," a girl replied.

"I doubt that too. Wasaibei can be a real dick," the guy said.

I was furious. Mo slandered me in an entire city and was making private things about me public. The worst part was that the people I now had to work with knew that Mo had access to my phone and that I wasn't able to say or do anything about it. Upon arriving home, I went straight into my room to google the possibilities and tools to hack an iPhone. I found absolutely nothing. I opened the iTunes app and pressed the AirPlay Icon. Two iPhones were listed in the device section. I took a screenshot of it and then called AppleCare. I told the woman from the hotline everything that had been going on with my phone. She assured me that it was impossible to hack an iPhone.

"But it is like someone is having a copy of my phone," I replied.

"Does someone have your Apple ID email and password?" the woman asked.

"I don't know. I hope not."

"If you really want to be safe, just change your Apple ID and password."

"But I have already done that, and when I reset my phone to factory settings, it asked me for the password for the other device," I replied.

"I am sorry. But this is your best option," she concluded.

I was getting desperate. How had Mo been able to gain access to the new phone? I did what the customer care had recommended me to do. Shortly after I had completed the process, I received a call from Unknown caller id. I picked up, but nobody answered. "How strange," I thought. After the call, I went out for a smoke. Brigitta and Mo were driving by my house.

"She looks great," I heard Brigitta say.

"Yes, I just want to destroy Sophie's beauty," Mo replied.

"So, that is why they are doing this. Because she is ugly, now they need to try to destroy my beauty so that Mo doesn't look like a complete moron dating her," I thought.

The next day, on the bus journey to the office, I took a screenshot of a wasabi pepper and edited it with a photo editing app. On top of it, I wrote: What do you associate WASAIBEI with." I saved the artwork to my image library. It was my only way to fight back and to check if Mo still had access to my phone. The Notes app opened again. Typed in was the word "wet". I was shacking with anger. "How the hell is he doing that?" I thought. This was a very funny game for Mo, but this man violated my privacy. I was very agitated by the time I arrived in Holborn. As I sat at my desk, I heard a girl say, 'What do you associate Wasaibei with.' She and her co-worker looked at their phone and then started laughing.

"Shh, she is looking over. I think she heard you," another girl said.

"She knows. If this would be happening to me, I would do something," the other girl said.

I was so enraged that I had to make a fist below my desk. "Yes, you would feel crap if someone would do that for you, but you still participate in it like it is an entertainment show," I thought furiously. I knew that if I said anything, I most likely would lose my job, but it was hard to deal with that mental torture. After work, I went into a pub and got myself one gin and tonic, for I felt the need to drown my feelings. It was like I had lost control over my life and felt, therefore, absolutely helpless. The people from the office knew what Mo was doing. They were aware of how devastating something like this must be, and they still took part in this cybercrime. It was humiliating and painful. In other words, it was cruel.

On the bus home, I got a text from a girl on Instagram. She told me that she had found my wallet. She was living in

Barnet as well, so we arranged that we would meet that evening in front of Tesco.

"Hi, are you Sophie?" a very pretty girl with black hair asked me.

"Yes, I am."

"I am Liza. I am the girl who found your wallet."

She took the wallet and gave it to me.

"I can't thank you enough," I said.

"No worries. It's just good karma. You do something nice for one person, and it will come back to you."

I insisted upon giving her ten pounds as a thank you. Later in the evening, I texted her on Instagram. I told her that if she ever wanted to do something with someone from Barnet, she just should send me a message.

CHAPTER 21

Liza texted back half an hour later and said she was free the following Saturday. Therefore, we arranged to meet in a pub in Barnet. It was something to look forward to and to keep me sane in an insane situation. I chose a very relaxed outfit that day, for I didn't want to appear as the kind of woman who craved constant attention from men. As soon as Liza entered the pub, I observed that she had also dressed casually. I considered this a good sign that sharing a similar style could be considered a similar mindset. It was a really fun evening. We talked about our careers, feminism and family. It was truly refreshing for a lot of women I had met only wanted to talk about guys. After half an hour in the pub, I saw Brigitta, who was in the company of another girl. She wore massive high heels, a red tank top and tight ripped jeans. If I hadn't known her, I would have assumed a hooker just had entered the pub. She looked at me and then left. I doubted that this was a coincidence, but I refused to let her ruin that evening for me.

Liza and I walked home together and were laughing about a funny story she told me about a previous housemate who had practised voodoo. Before we parted, Liza and I exchanged phone numbers. Just as I had saved her number in the Contact app, the Notes app opened. Typed in was the letter A. A black BMW drove by at precisely that moment; as I had seen Mo and Brigitta in that car before, I had to assume it was them. I kept my emotions under control and wished Liza a goodnight. At home, I opened the Urban dictionary website. According to the site, 'A' meant 'The thing that's stalking the girls on pretty little liars by sending them creepy texts.' It was absolutely insane.

The following Wednesday, Nathalie asked me if I had heard of the Coronavirus.

"Those are news to me."

She laughed.

"It is big news. People are really worried and fear that they could die," she replied.

I wasn't too concerned, for the story with Mo was way more stressful for me. Later in the evening, I was reading in my room. "Finally, I can relax and breathe through," I thought while turning the page.

"He said that Sophie is crazy and that he offered us eighteen-thousand if we will help him to get rid of her," I heard Josh say to Nathalie.

This was too much for me. The next day, I called in sick, for I had decided to go to the police with the little evidence that I had. I was scared on the way, for I feared what Mo would do to me when he would find out that I intended to report him. I told the police everything that had occurred between Mo and me, except the fact that I once had called him a stupid Muslim. Although I knew that I only had texted Mo that because I had been rightfully angry, I didn't feel comfortable sharing it with the police, for they could consider the comment as racist. I informed them that Mo had been driving by my house and told the officers what had been typed into my phone. One officer said that it was a cybercrime and unlawful stalking but that it would be very hard to proof. The other police officer said that the case was worth investigating, for there was the possibility that Mo might kill me. They informed me that someone would be in touch in a couple of days to give me an update on the investigation.

Later in the day, I got an email from my manager. They were concerned about my symptoms, for they feared it might be Coronavirus. Therefore, I wasn't able to attend work the following day. "I fucking hate Mo. This is all his fault, and now I even miss work because of him," I thought. I had to check with a hotline and get a confirmation that it wasn't coronavirus before I was able to return to the office. The confirmation from NHS 111 that my symptoms were not consistent with Coronavirus was sufficient for my employer to return to my workplace on Monday.

I was determined to put extra effort into my tasks to compensate for the time I had been absent.

"She went to the police," I heard a girl say.

"Yes, he is actually really scared now," another girl replied.

"Yeah, he said that she is not worth going to jail for," the other one replied.

I was something between furious, satisfied and hopeful. I was furious that they were talking like this about me and satisfied that Mo was scared. Whatever Mo was doing, it was very much illegal. I was aware that I didn't have enough proof, but I still hoped that the police would investigate Mo anyway and that justice would be done. The following day after work, I got a call from the police. The officer informed me that I didn't have enough evidence and that they didn't even have Mo's address. Therefore, they were not able to pursue the case. I was desperate. Mo was causing me so much stress, and by the look of it, nobody was able or willing to help me. He made me uncomfortable everywhere I was. I didn't even have peace at home because Mo had contacted

Nathalie and Josh as well. I wanted to put an end to it, even when that meant that I had to kill Mo.

The next day, however, the only subject people were discussing was Coronavirus. Everybody was really scared. Everybody except me. The virus was nothing in comparison to the terror inflicted upon me by a sick psychopath. In the morning, we were informed that the management was talking about the necessity to work from home. By the end of the day, they had made their decision. We all got an email informing us that we should take our equipment with us and not return to the office the next day. It put my mind at ease that I could work remotely, for it would be much easier to concentrate. In the evening, we saw the government announcement on TV, which declared the first lockdown. Most people were probably sad about it. I was grateful for it was an escape from Mo's psycho terror. I went to Costa to get myself for the last time a cappuccino. The coffee shop was almost empty. I talked to the barista about the lockdown. She was scared, for she didn't know how she would be able to afford the rent. I felt sorry for those people, but Coronavirus was a life saver for me. Furthermore, for the first time in my life, I was lucky to still have a good job.

The following morning, I went out for a walk. The park was empty. I felt so much safer now because I knew Mo could no longer follow me. Nathalie and Josh weren't able to work anymore, but I was, and I loved it. I knew that Mo had contacted Josh and Nathalie and that they knew that it was illegal to gain access to a phone without the owner's consent. Nathalie had not reported Mo to the police, and I could no longer think good of her. Nathalie had told me about Buddhism and karma. I hoped very much that every single one of them would one day get their karma for doing this to me.

My job was fun and creative, and working from home was pure joy. I was able to focus and perform well as I no longer had to listen to people's gossip. At least I was able to think that for a short period. Just a couple of days after the lockdown announcement, I saw Josh talking to someone on the phone.

"What if she dies now and I have done this?" I heard Mo say.

"Don't worry about it. She is never sober. She is really not worth caring about," Josh replied.

I was furious. I hadn't been drinking in a while, and when I had consumed alcohol, I had to relief the stress caused by this insane cruelty. Mo's response I wasn't able to hear.

"So, the only thing I must do is plug it in?" Josh asked Mo.

"Yes," he replied.

The conversation between Mo and Josh made me feel

trapped in a cage, for I wasn't even able to confront Josh. It was lockdown, and if I had faced him, he probably would have denied it, or Nathalie would have been able to ask me to leave the house. The next day, I went out for a smoke. When I came back, I saw Josh coming out of my room. He was actually grinning. I guessed that he had been there to perform the task Mo had asked him to do. In the afternoon, I walked past the living room. Josh had his headphones on and said very loud, 'Wow. This is absolutely incredible.'

"Shhhhhh, she will hear you," Nathalie told him.

I found that very bizarre. Why had Nathalie been worried that I could have heard that?

Later in the evening, I thought that Josh and Nathalie would pay the price for this crime one day. I counted on karma to punish them for helping Mo.

"She thinks now that we are evil and will be punished by karma," I heard Josh say to Nathalie.

They were laughing. Was Josh able to hear my thoughts? How could something like this be possible?

"She is aware that I can hear her thoughts," he said.

I took out my phone and googled telepathy. There was no plausible information to be found on the internet that would have provided an explanation for this. Was I simply losing my mind? A couple of days later, I heard Nathalie screaming in the living room at six in the morning. She was hysterical. I went there and saw that Josh was trying to calm her down.

"What is going on?" I asked.

"Her brother died. Please get out so I can take care of her," he replied.

I went back into my room.

"I just tried to help Sophie," I heard Nathalie say through the walls of my room.

It was a very odd thing to say in such a moment. It was difficult for me to feel sorry for Nathalie. She knew it was wrong not to report Mo to the police. I thought that Nathalie had said that because she considered the death of her brother as the punishment of the Universe for participation in a cruel crime. Deep down inside, she must have felt guilty. Although Nathalie had done wrong, I felt pity for her after my anger had evaporated, for I knew how hard it was to lose a family member. After two hours I went in there. Nathalie was still crying but appeared to have better control over herself.

"I am very sorry for your loss," I said.

"Thank you," she replied.

CHAPTER 22

I was certain that Nathalie and Josh would recognize that karma was real after the sad news of her brother's death. Nathalie was an educated woman, and therefore, I was convinced that she would see the error of her ways. Very soon afterwards, I was proved wrong. Through the walls of my room, I overheard Josh telling Nathalie about everything I was thinking. I often observed that Josh stepped outside the house to have phone conversations, which could only mean he didn't want to be overheard.

"He said that she is crazy and that he only wants to help Sophie," I heard Josh say to Nathalie two weeks after her brother had died.

"I don't believe this. People are going through things. That doesn't make them crazy," she replied.

"He offers us lots of money," Josh replied without

bothering to keep his voice down.

I couldn't take this anymore. "So, I am the crazy one because I sent Mo a couple of messages, and he is the sane one, although he is stalking me," I thought furiously while smoking a cigarette. Was this the new definition of sanity? Stalking, cyber bullying, slander and getting illegal access to a phone? I was in disbelief, but maybe there was a very simple explanation for Josh's desire to support Mo. Money. It was transparent that Mo's offer appealed to Josh. I would never have been tempted to participate in a crime simply because of money, but I was aware that not everyone was thinking along that line.

The laundry room was down stairs next to Nathalie's bedroom. One night, I had to go down there to get my cloths out of the dryer.

"Is it ok when I come down," I asked from the top of the stairs.

"Sure, no problem," Nathalie replied.

As soon as I reached the end of the staircase, I saw that Josh was in bed with Nathalie and that they were both half-naked. Too appalled to speak, I took my clothes and went back to my room. "Oh, my god. Was that what I think it was?" I asked myself. A couple of days later, I went into the living room and saw Nathalie leaning over Josh. He had no shirt on, and she was showing him her breasts. When she saw me, she closed her dressing gown. I was sickened. "And this people have the audacity to suggest that I am crazy," I thought.

Liza texted me a day later to enquire if I wanted to join her and her sister for a picnic in the park. I was more than happy to and was thrilled that I finally would be able to talk to someone sane. We arranged to meet at Tesco the following Saturday at two in the afternoon. Liza introduced me to her sister, Jennifer, who was very cheerful and good-natured. I liked her immediately. We bought food and of course drinks. On the way to the park, we encountered Josh.

"Hi," he said.

"Hi," I replied.

"He is very handsome," Liza said once he was out of earshot.

I told them that I had seen Josh and Nathalie half-naked in bed together and that they shared the same bed every night.

"Oh, my god. That's incest," Jennifer said.

"You don't know that for sure," Liza replied.

"Come on. It almost certainly is," Jennifer declared determined.

We talked about it a lot while we were sitting and drinking in the park. Other topics we discussed that afternoon were, of course, guys and the pandemic. After two hours, we ran out of alcohol, so we had to go back to the shop to get some more.

"I really need to go the toilet," Jennifer said.

"We can go to my place. It's just on the way back to the park," I replied.

They wanted to have a look at Josh and Nathalie when we went inside. So, I offered them a glass of water. When we entered the kitchen, I saw that Nathalie looked uncomfortable. Therefore, we didn't stay long. We returned to the park, where we drank, laughed and talked. Jennifer was convinced that Nathalie was sleeping with Josh. Liza wasn't entirely sure. Whatever the truth was, it gave us plenty to talk and speculate about. The evening was highly entertaining. After all this time in lockdown, we were finally able to have some fun. At ten, I returned home. Although I had consumed many gins and tonics during the day, I didn't really feel drunk. Nathalie was chanting when I entered the living room. Josh was sitting at the dining table. I went into the kitchen and was in great need of water. "How sick can you be if you sleep with your son?" I thought. I heard that Nathalie had stopped chanting and walked over to Josh.

"She is just trying to bring you up against me," Nathalie said to Josh while I was standing in the kitchen.

"Enough is enough," I thought. The next day, I looked for a room on the internet. It didn't take me long to find something I liked. I called the woman who had advertised the room and arranged a viewing for the following day.

"She wants to move out," I heard Josh say to Nathalie through the walls of my room.

"You need to talk to her. If she moves out, I won't have enough money," she said.

"What should I say to her?" Josh replied.

"Haha, serves you right," I thought. They were talking about me, although they knew that I could hear them. They didn't care how their behaviour and their participation in a cybercrime affected me. I was delighted that Nathalie would face the consequences for their wrong doings.

The next day, I took the bus to my potential new home. I noticed that the area was much prettier than the one I was currently living in. "The new place can't be worse than Nathalie's place," I thought before I rang the doorbell. A small woman with grey hair opened the door.

"Hi, I am Hazel."

"I am Sophie. It's nice to meet you."

"Likewise, come on in."

The house was stunning. As a matter of fact, it was the most beautiful house I had seen in my entire life. It had a massive kitchen and a massive living room. It was modern and very stylishly decorated. The garden was delightful, for it had palm trees and a big patio. The bedroom wasn't that big but very stylish and had an ensuite bathroom. It was like a dream after a nightmare. After Hazel had shown me the house, we sat in the garden and talked. She was nothing else but cool. She asked me why I wanted to move out of my current place. So, I told her that I had seen Josh and Nathalie half-naked in bed together.

"Oh, my god," she said.

"So, you think it was incest as well?" I asked.

"Oh yes. Definitely. You are doing the right thing to get away from that situation."

Hazel was more than happy to give me the room, and we arranged that I would move in the following Saturday. Back home, I immediately informed Nathalie.

"Can't you wait a couple of months until you move out? If you move out now, we will struggle financially," she said.

"I am sorry that you are financially not stable, but this is not my problem. I am not happy in this house anymore and found a place I like."

Josh joined the conversation and tried to argue with me.

"I am sorry, but I made my decision."

"You are being very selfish. You act like you are a good person, but you're not," Nathalie said to me.

This woman has some nerve. She knew about cybercrime and that Mo was stalking me and she didn't report him to the police, and now she was telling me that I was a bad person because I was no longer willing to put up with it.

"I am sorry you feel that way," I replied and walked away.

I was rather proud of myself at that moment because I thought I had behaved very classy. Back in my room, I overheard Josh talking to someone.

"She said that you and your mother committed incest," Mo said loud enough for me to hear him.

"That's not true. She is lying. You are right. She is crazy," Josh replied.

"Now she will be moving into a stunning house because of you," Mo complained.

"It wasn't because of me. Just give me the money."

"They are insane," I concluded.

By Saturday morning, I had packed everything. I gave Nathalie the keys back and hoped I would never have to see her again. Once again, I took an Uber and arrived at Hazel's house twenty minutes later. Hazel was very sweet. She was not the youngest anymore, but she helped me to move everything into my room. Once I had unpacked, I joined her in the garden for a smoke. I told her about Nathalie's and Josh's reactions.

"It's very good that you moved out of that house. You will see. You will do very well here," she replied.

I felt like I had been reborn. The beauty of the house and garden helped me to relax. Close by were two lovely parks where I could go for a walk in the morning. Cooking was also more enjoyable in that beautiful, clean kitchen, and I began to live much healthier. Preparing my meals in Nathalie's house had not been a pleasant experience, for the kitchen always had been a mess, which, in my opinion, just showed how selfish Nathalie and Josh were. Hazel was a great housemate. She was kind, interesting to talk to and quite often a lot of fun.

"He said that he would not sleep with me as long as Sophie is living in this house," I suddenly heard Brigitta's voice say in my head on the second day.

Shock paralyzed me for a brief moment. "Am I going insane? What is happening?" I thought. Was Brigitta perhaps able to communicate telepathically? Afterall, I had heard Josh talking about my thoughts. After two weeks, Hazel told me that a guy would come the following day to look at the other available room. The news was far from being welcome to me. Everything was perfect the way it was, and I was therefore concerned that a new tenant could disrupt the peace of the house. I was working when he arrived. As I was curious, I went into the garden for a smoke. He was a very handsome guy who had light chocolate brown skin and dark long curls.

"Hi, I am Sophie."

"Dimitri," he replied.

He gave me a searching look. Hazel, Dimitri and I talked

about the pandemic and how it had impacted our lives. Dimitri was fun to talk to, but something didn't feel right. I couldn't say exactly what it was. After one hour of chatting, he informed Hazel that he would like to take the room.

"Cute, isn't he?" Hazel said to me once Dimitri had left.

Dimitri moved in on the weekend. Hazel cooked a beautiful dinner to welcome him and me to the house. He talked a lot about music and, in general, appeared to be an interesting person. The feeling that something was not right, however, didn't vanish. The one thing I learned from the story with Mo was never to discredit my own gut feeling. I thought that I would keep that in mind. Dimitri was away the next day and the day after. When I considered that we were still in the lockdown period and the rent was six hundred a month, I regarded his constant absence as odd. Hazel appeared to be bedazzled with him. Both Hazel and Dimitri had a lot more free time than myself, as I was the only one who was still working. From my window, I often observed them talking together in the garden.

"Sophie is very beautiful. Isn't she?" Hazel asked Dimitri one day.

"She is," Dimitri replied.

"I fear that it might complicate the situation in this house," Hazel said.

I thought that Hazel was scared that I would begin a

romantic relationship with Dimitri and assumed that she was concerned that she would feel like the third wheel if that would happen. I was certainly able to comprehend that concern of hers, but I still didn't appreciate that she was talking like this about me, for it made me worry.

The next day, I went out for a walk. When I came back, I encountered Dimitri alone in the kitchen. He said hello to me. I was listening to some music and wanted to put my phone away in order to be able to talk to him. The Notes app opened and typed in was again some rubbish. I let out a sound of exhaustion.

"What's up with you?" Dimitri asked.

"It's complicated."

"Does some guy not leave you alone?"

"In some way."

"Come on. Tell me," he said.

He insisted upon it, and therefore, I told him the full story. I couldn't quite read his facial expression.

"That's so messed up."

I thought 'messed up' didn't describe the situation accurately. For me, Mo was a sick psychopath. Messed up was, therefore, the understatement of the century. Dimitri urged me to tell Hazel. I was by no means keen on it, for it was a lot easier for every party if people didn't know what Mo was doing to me. "If I don't tell Hazel, Dimitri will," I concluded inside my head.

"This is sick. You need to go to the police," Hazel said once I had finished my story.

"I have already done that. They didn't consider the evidence as sufficient."

"Doesn't matter. You need to go there again and again until they take you seriously."

I knew that the police wouldn't investigate Mo for the evidence I had was inadequate. Resetting my phone had turned out to be pointless as well. I already had tried it a couple of times. The problem didn't appear to have a solution, and therefore, I deeply regretted that I had talked about it. I decided to wait and see if I would be able to collect some more evidence before reporting to Mo again. Hazel informed us that she would be away on a girls' trip the following weekend. Dimitri, therefore, suggested that we would celebrate our freedom with a bottle of gin.

"Sounds like a plan," I replied.

On Friday, Hazel left the house early in the morning, and Dimitri was away the entire day. After work, I sat in the garden, drank a gin and tonic and smoked a cigarette. The day had lacked excitement, and therefore, I wondered when Dimitri would return. I ordered an Indian takeaway and then began to watch a movie.

"You look very sweaty," I said to Dimitri when he entered

the kitchen half an hour later.

"Yeah, I had Jujutsu training and didn't take a shower yet."

"Jujutsu? Cool."

"I brought something for you."

He had a bottle of gin in his hand.

"Nice," I replied.

"Yeah, now you will get a proper gin and tonic"

I laughed.

"A proper gin and tonic?" I asked.

"Yep, you will see."

He made one for me and one for himself.

"Very nice," I said after I took the first sip.

"I told you."

We went into the garden. I smoked a cigarette, and he a joint.

"Does that guy still bother you?" he asked.

"Nothing happened since we last spoke about it."

"Good, maybe he gave up."

"Maybe," I replied, but I seriously doubted it.

Mo was a psychopath, and he wanted to make me pay for the rejection and the rude messages I had sent him. We went back into the living room and watched a movie. Dimitri gazed at me quite a few times. I saw that we both were thinking about the same thing. Then he kissed me. It felt good and exciting. We started touching each other.

"Do you want to go to the bedroom?" he asked.

"I do," I replied.

Dimitri was laying on top of me and kissed me passionately.

"Oh, my god. This is real. Doesn't Sophie realize that we can see her," I heard Brigitta say in my head.

"Achh," came from Mo.

I thought that I had too much gin and, therefore, ignored it. Dimitri and I continued. He took off my cloths and touched me passionately.

We woke up late the next day. I went down to the kitchen and made myself a cup of coffee, which I took with me into the garden. I put the coffee cup and my phone on the table. Dimitri joined me just when I had lighted a cigarette.

"Hi, beautiful. How did you sleep?" he asked.

"Really good. And you?"

Suddenly, the Notes app opened and typed in the word 'Slag'. I looked the word up on Urban dictionary. It meant whore. I wasn't able to hide something like this, and therefore, I told Dimitri about it.

"I know an app developer. I will call this guy right now and ask him if he can figure out how that guy got access to your phone."

"OK," I replied.

He indeed called his friend and elaborated on everything I had told him. I observed Dimitri feeling anxious.

"So, the phone is cloned, and he has installed spyware?" Dimitri said while giving me a concerned look.

I didn't hear his friend's reply, which I considered weird as I always had heard Mo talking to Josh.

"How long does it take to clone a phone?" he asked.

I tried hard to listen to his friend's response but couldn't understand a word.

"Just a couple of seconds?" Dimitri then said while looking at me, very worried. "So, he is able to hear everything we say and able to see what we are doing right now?"

I didn't wait for the response, for I no longer had any doubt that Mo had been spying on me from the moment I had rejected him. All pointed in that direction. He had shown up twice when I had been on a date with Tim. How else would he have been able to know my location? I went into the garden, for I never had needed a cigarette more than I did at that moment. In order to release the stress, I walked up and down. I couldn't get one clear thought because the disturbing revelation had shocked me like nothing had ever shocked me before. Dimitri had followed me.

"Are you ok?" he asked.

"Am I ok? Are you serious? No. I am fucking not ok. This psycho has been spying on me for I don't know how long.

He probably has seen us having sex. So, no. I am not ok."

He had an odd expression on his face.

"Fuck it. Fuck him."

"Fuck it? For me, this is horrible," I yelled.

"I get that, but now you know how he has done it. You are able to do something about it. You might even be able to get him arrested because it's illegal to clone a phone."

"I already went to the police. They said that I don't have enough evidence."

"Just go again. Tell them they have to take this seriously," he concluded.

"You know what? You are right. I will go to the police on Monday, but I won't let him ruin our weekend."

"That's the spirit," Dimitri replied.

He and I spent the whole weekend together. My phone stayed turned off, and I made sure that it wasn't anywhere near me. Although I had said I wouldn't let Mo ruin my weekend, my mind wasn't free anymore, for Mo and Brigitta were literally in my head. Hazel came back on Sunday.

"Welcome back. How was your trip?" I asked, noticing that I wasn't really capable anymore of being interested in someone else, for my mind was grievously troubled.

"We had an amazing time. How was your weekend?" she replied.

It was Dimitri, however, who replied. He told her what we

had found out.

"Oh, my god. This sick. But you can do something about it now," she said.

I called work the next day and said that I needed the day off for a personal reason. Afterwards, I went to the police. They told me that I would have to report it as a cybercrime. They gave me the contact details and informed me that this was my best chance. I went home and did precisely that. It was a nightmare, and I wished I had never met Mo.

"You should probably get a new phone and number," Dimitri said when I was done.

"Do you really think it wise to do that before the police have investigated him?" I asked.

"You should. It will give you peace of mind. There is no chance that he will be able to get back in. You should reset your MacBook as well. Just make sure that you back everything up."

I nodded. It was so much trouble. I hated Mo like I had never hated anyone before. The next day, I took the afternoon off to get a new phone and number.

"I did it," I said when I got home.

"Good for you, Sophie. Now you are rid of him," Hazel said.

For three days, it was very quiet and normal after that. I kept spending time with Dimitri. Hazel began to notice that something was going on between me and him.

"We will kill him if you continue seeing him," I heard Brigitta say in my head.

Was I crazy? Was this real? I was concerned for Dimitri's safety and, therefore, told him that Mo had been able to get back into my phone and that he had said that he would kill him if I would continue seeing him. The fact that I was hearing voices inside my head, I kept to myself. Naturally, I was worried that someone would think that I was crazy. Dimitri called a couple of people, packed his stuff and left the house. I didn't see him for two weeks after that. The situation was disturbing and devastating. Alcohol became my medicine for the effects of that psycho-terror. The only other solution would have been to kill Mo and Brigitta, but a voice inside of me was telling me that they were not worth a jail sentence.

A couple of days later, I released my anger by yelling in my room. Hazel was not in the house, and therefore, I had no concern that someone would witness this tantrum.

"You fucking psycho. I hate you," I shouted, knowing that they would be able to hear me, for they had installed spyware in my phone.

"Oh, my god. She is serious," I heard Brigitta say in my head.

I completely lost it.

"Serious? How could anyone love Mo? He is an insane,

cruel, pathetic psychopath. He is just with you, Brigitta because you're the ugliest woman in the world. A beautiful, kind woman would never stay with such a monster," I screamed and was super glad that nobody could hear me talking to a phantom.

"Yeah, your face is really shit," Brigitta screamed inside my head.

"My face is shit? Even Mo once dumped you because you were too ugly for him," I replied.

Shouting at them hadn't made me feel any better. Quite the opposite. The anger and hate got only worse and made my muscles painfully contract. I walked to the closest shop and bought several gin and tonic cans. On the way back, I saw Mo driving by me.

"When you didn't want me, why did you send me those texts?" he yelled from his car.

I was too shocked to say something at first. How could all this be real?

"Why did I send you those texts? Because you're a sick psycho, and I would have done anything to push you away," I thought.

"You did want Mo," I heard Brigitta say in my head.

"We can't all be as pathetic as you are. I would never go out with an ugly, abusive, insane, stalking psycho like you do," I replied, fully aware that I was only repeating myself.

I didn't hear anything after that. "Get the fuck out of my life," I thought.

"Sophie would miss me when I would stop now. I will continue," Mo said.

"You only want to continue because you know that bitch is too ugly for you," I thought.

"I love Brigitta. I wanted Sophie to want me," I heard him say in my head.

I was shaking with anger, hate and pain.

"You know Sophie. Brigitta asked me to see you. That's why I asked you out," Mo said.

It was unimaginable. "How can this be real? How can someone communicate into the head of another person?" I thought. Mo and Brigitta kept talking into my head every day from then on. I had more tantrums in my room because I wasn't able to keep the anger bottled up. Dimitri informed Hazel that he wanted to move out because of the situation. He gave her one month's notice. Hazel was not happy about it at all. I felt horrible. It was like Mo had taken everything away from me, and I was not able to do anything about it. I was in this beautiful house with great people around me and a cool job, but I couldn't enjoy one minute.

Not long after that, the compass in Photoshop on my work MacBook Pro started to flash up. This demonstrated that Mo had cloned or had asked someone who had been living with me to clone this device as well. It was way too much to handle. I screamed and kicked the walls. After I had given my feelings air, I went into the garden for a smoke. Hazel, who apparently had heard me yelling, asked me what was wrong. I told her that Mo had been able to get access to my work computer. She left without saying a word. One hour later, she told me that she wanted me out of the house.

CHAPTER 23

I didn't know how many gins and tonics I had after Hazel had given me notice, but it had been too many. The situation was overwhelmingly stressful, infuriating and painful. I looked again at the spare room, but it was very difficult, for I hardly had any money. My budget allowed me only to pay three hundred pounds for the deposit. Only one room was advertised that fitted in that price category. The place was in Cockfosters.

"Ha, Sophie can only afford to pay three hundred pounds," Brigitta said.

"I wonder what people would think about Brigitta when one day her true character is revealed to the world," I thought.

I called the guy who had advertised the room early in the morning, the day after Hazel had told me that she wanted me out of the house. We arranged that I would view the room the very same day. It wasn't very pretty, but I knew I had no choice. I said that I would take it.

Afterwards, I started training in Kung Fu and Karate.

"I will kill you, Mo, and will kill that ugly bitch of yours," I said inside my head.

"If you murder Brigitta, we will kill you," Mo said in my head.

"I don't care. You deserve to die for what you did to me," I thought.

"Well, Sophie doesn't know where we live," Mo said.

"True, but I know where you work," I replied.

"Yeah, you are right. It's good that Sophie doesn't know where we live. When she would see our house, she would be so jealous," Brigitta said.

I wasn't scared, for I was so angry that the consequences of murder appeared to be a fair price for getting Mo and Brigitta out of my life forever. I practised kata's, all kinds of kicks and punches. The movie 'The Karate Kid' was a huge inspiration for me during that time. One day, I practised balance on the bench in Hazel's Garden.

"She is standing on the edge of a bench," Mo said into my head.

"How on earth can they see me? Are there cameras somewhere," I thought. I heard Brigitta laugh.

"She thinks that we have installed cameras," she said.

Every time I heard their voices inside my head, I became angrier. Hazel observed me on several occasions training in the garden. She looked worried. I was able to guess that she suspected that I intended to attack Mo and Brigitta. Hazel's wish to have me out of the house was understandable, but that didn't make it easier. The situation was not my fault, and I felt like everyone acted like it was. "If this would happen to them, they would have tantrums in their rooms, and they would have the desire to kill Mo and Brigitta as well," I thought furiously. Everyone wanted to be rid of the problem, but nobody wanted to help solve it. "The people who have evidence should report Mo and Brigitta. Why will nobody help?" I thought desperately. I moved out two weeks later. Hazel and I parted on good terms. I assured her that I understood her and didn't bear her ill will, for it was obvious that Hazel genuinely felt sorry for me.

"Sophie doesn't know that we created a trap for her in the new place," Brigitta said when I was in the Uber.

By the time I arrived at Cockfosters, I was in such a state of anxiety that I was trembling all over my body. After I had unpacked all my stuff, I went out for a drink in a bar close to Trent Park. Shortly after I had taken my seat outside, I saw Brigitta and Mo. Brigitta was easy to recognize, for she wore a unique, floral silk blouse I had seen many times on her while

I had been working at CooperateEvent. Shock paralyzed me because I couldn't comprehend how they had courageously shown their ugly faces. At the moment I had decided to go after them, they were out of sight. Two girls were walking past me and starred at me without shame.

"There she is," the girl said.

This statement was sufficient to conclude that Mo and Brigitta made private things about me public to a broad audience. My body and mind were overwhelmed with that revelation. In the evening, I took my phone out with me and acted like I was having a phone conversation.

"Get the hell out of my life. I will kill you if you don't leave me alone," I said.

Mo and Brigitta were, without any doubt, able to hear me as they had apparently installed spyware in my phone. However, I had said too many times already that I would kill them without taking any action to do it. It was essential to say it out loud, however. Only thinking about it was driving me insane. I didn't hear anything that evening. The next morning, I woke up early to practice Kung Fu outside my house.

"She is training," Mo said inside my head.

"Leave me alone, or I will kill you," I thought.

"Maybe we should leave," Mo said.

"If we leave now, everyone will see Sophie as better than me. Do you want that, Mo?" Brigitta said in a whining voice, which woke the desire inside of me to strangle her with my bare hands.

"You know, Sophie, Brigitta asked me to see you, and we asked Dimitri to see you as well. He only moved into Hazel's house because we asked him to," Mo said.

"Sophie can never know that we recorded her while she was having sex with him," Brigitta communicated.

Tears came into my eyes, but my anger exceeded my pain at that moment. "I will have my revenge. In this life or the next," I thought. Mo had confirmed that he had planned this from the beginning because Brigitta had feared that other people would consider me better than her. After work, I was no longer able to hide my sadness. I cried, and I couldn't stop crying. "There is no way out of this situation. If I really kill Mo and Brigitta, I will land in jail. No matter what I do, I can't win," I thought. Suicide seemed to be, at that moment, the only answer for a problem that appeared to have no solution. I went into the kitchen and took a kitchen knife. Back in my room, I tried to cut my wrist, but the knife was not nearly sharp enough. After fifteen minutes of pressing down the knife on my wrist, I saw that there was no point and, therefore, went outside for a smoke.

"You are hurting me so much that I want to take my own life," I said quietly.

"Oh, Sophie. We never wanted to hurt you," Brigitta said

in my head.

"You never wanted to hurt me? Mo said you asked him to see me! You stalk me, and you don't stop, although you made me suicidal. You keep going. Now you want to make people believe that it wasn't your intention to cause me pain."

"Well, it's Sophie's fault. She should not have tried to be better than me," Brigitta said.

Furious, I went back into my room and changed into a workout outfit. Five minutes later, I was back in front of the house and trained like a maniac.

"You were hurting Brigitta," Mo said.

"With what? By taking a selfie or because I didn't want her pathetic boyfriend," I thought.

"You will bow to Brigitta," Mo said when I was practising my kicks.

Something inside me switched. I felt stronger.

"I am not bowing down to an ugly, mean, insane, cruel, talent-free bitch, who is so pathetic and has such low self-esteem that she has it necessary to ask her boyfriend to see other women," I said to him inside my head.

"Ahhhhhhh," Brigitta was screaming.

It was a triumph. For the first time, I had succeeded in hurting Brigitta back. Apparently, I had hit a nerve, for Brigitta was obviously aware that she was neither beautiful, talented, intelligent or kind.

"Don't worry, Brigitta. I will have Sophie see me," Mo declared.

"You're right. Then everyone will see me as better," Brigitta communicated.

"Do you really think, Brigitta, that anyone will see you as better? You are a disgusting person who dates a moron. You want to destroy other women so that you can feel good about yourself. Do you really think that there is just one woman in this world who could think good of you? There are a lot of women who fight for women's rights. You drag all those women down by encouraging your pathetic boyfriend to harass and abuse other women. You even asked him to see other women so that he would dump them afterwards. You are a disgrace," I said. "And you, Mo. You said that you are a good Muslim, but you are the worst. You demonstrate that you use your religion as an excuse to harass and abuse. There are good Muslims in this world. Guys like you give the good ones a bad name. People are prejudiced because of people like you. And you have the nerve to say that I discriminated against you? Pointing out that harassment and abuse are wrong is not racism. People are prejudiced because they are afraid that they get hurt, and its people like you that demonstrate that there is indeed a reason to be scared," I added.

When I went out for a smoke the next morning, I saw that

Brigitta and Mo had parked in front of my house. It was unbelievable.

"There she is," Mo said.

They drove off immediately. "You are such a coward," I thought. Later in the day, the compass in Photoshop started flashing up. Without a doubt Mo wanted to distract me from doing my job. "Is that guy not working anymore?" I thought. I googled him and Brigitta. On LinkedIn, I saw that Brigitta was no longer working for CooperateEvent and Mo was no longer employed at the design agency. They both had stopped working in the same month that I had threatened to kill them. Either they both had been made redundant, or they both had resigned because they wanted to stalk me. It was absolutely insane. "How are they able to hear my thoughts, and how the hell do they manage to communicate into my head?" I thought.

"Ha, she wants to know how we did," Brigitta said.

I researched for hours if there was a technology out there which made it possible to hear someone's thoughts and to communicate into someone's brain. Some companies were working on it, but nothing had been publicized that would have illuminated this bizarre situation. Schizophrenia or psychosis certainly would have been an explanation, but I doubted it, for Josh had been able to hear my thoughts as well. I had heard him talk about what I had been thinking many times. Mo and Brigitta were somehow able to read my mind. I was certain of it. I tried to control my thoughts. For a couple of days, I succeeded, but Mo kept flashing up the compass in Photoshop.

"I want to hear what she is thinking," Brigitta declared.

I didn't want to give her that pleasure any more, but then I snapped.

"You are only doing this to me because you are the ugliest woman. You are ugly because you have an ugly heart. You are afraid that people will see me as better than you because you know what a shitty personality you got. Deep down, you know that you are worthless because you know it's known it's not about what someone looks like or who they date. It's about what kind of character a person has," I said.

"You have to send Zane there. He can kill her," she said to Mo.

"I can't get her killed. What would people say," Mo replied.

"If you don't send Zane there, then everyone will see her as better than me," Brigitta said.

"I will have her see me," Mo replied.

"How do you want to do that?" Brigitta asked.

"I will send Zane there. He will bring her to me," Mo said.

"You are an insane, evil monster. Send Zane here. I will kill anyone who tries to help you, and it will be called self-defence," I replied.

I trained harder, and my Kung Fu skills increased rapidly. It made me less fearful, but I always looked over my shoulder from the day Brigitta had expressed her wish to have me killed. Mo and Brigitta were, without any doubt, insane. Whether they were able to communicate telepathically or not, they were definitively stalking me twenty-four hours a day. I wasn't able to understand how anyone could like a woman like Brigitta. She asked her boyfriend to sleep with other women, and when they didn't want him, she asked him to stalk them.

"You are not even worth the crime. You are just an insane, ugly, psycho bitch. I won't kill you," I told Brigitta.

"We will see about this. Nobody will see you as better than me," Brigitta said.

"You're crazy. If you were a nice and sane person, you wouldn't be that scared that everyone would see me as better than you. You are terrified because you are horrible. You need to destroy my reputation because you don't want people to notice your dreadful character," I replied.

"Don't worry, Brigitta. I will go there tomorrow. Then people will know that she would try to kill me," Mo said.

The next day, I saw Mo walking by my house. He looked hideous. I once had considered Mo as half-way handsome. Now, he was the ugliest man in the world in my eyes. At that moment, I was very ashamed that I once had kissed him. Retaliation was no longer a desire of mine because I was aware that Mo was only walking by my house because he anticipated a reaction. He wanted to terrorize and torture me into madness in order to make me look unstable, and himself look good. I went into my room and looked at images of him and Brigitta on Flickr and Instagram. I began to laugh and couldn't stop. "I totally get why Mo is doing this to me. He goes out with one of the ugliest and most pathetic women I have ever seen. No wonder he was trying to destroy other women; otherwise, he would look like a joke dating Brigitta," I thought. I kept laughing and couldn't stop.

"She is just laughing because she wants me," Mo said.

"You think you are pretty, Sophie. But you are not. Cameras and mirrors don't tell the truth," Brigitta said.

I was now rolling on the ground with laughter. Mo started to flash up the compass again on the cloned company MacBook. How was that guy able to think that I could want him? He was clearly delusional.

"You are nothing else but an ugly psychopath, Mo. No other woman, but this ugly bitch Brigitta, could ever want or like you," I repeated in my head.

"We will see about this," Brigitta replied.

I started to get a very bad feeling. The possibility was there that Brigitta might have asked Mo to do this to other women as well. She certainly was capable and ruthless enough for it. I remembered that Ugne had said she had been devastated because of Mo and thought that this probably wasn't the first time they had done something like this.

CHAPTER 24

Mo and Brigitta wanted me to attack them. If I had granted them their wish, I would have been labelled as crazy. Any act of violence on my side would also have enabled them to press charges against me. Murder, although certainly desirable in specific moments, would have had the consequence that my life would have been over, for I would have spent the rest of my life in jail. The police would have needed more evidence, and therefore, I was not able to do anything. It was driving me crazy that they wouldn't face the consequences of their crime. With sufficient evidence, a cybercrime of that nature would have resulted in a one to five years prison sentence. "Why can't the police get the evidence? This is their goddam responsibility," I thought furiously.

Focusing on my job and practising Kung Fu were certainly powerful distractions, but Mo was relentless. He repeated, "I will have Sophie see me" a hundred times daily. I tried to block it out with music, but it was nearly impossible. When I ignored him, he kept flashing up the compass on the cloned company MacBook. I began to sing in my room, but I couldn't hear myself, for I had the headphones on. As Mo and Brigitta were able to listen in, I hoped that my voice sounded terrible enough to torture them. A part of that singing helped me to release my emotions in a constructive way, no matter how good or bad my voice was.

Some days, I was mentally stable. On other days, I cracked and drank heavily. On my worst days, I cried and wanted to take my own life. "I will not let Mo destroy me. I will find a way to get rid of him," I thought, determined. I found sufficient information on the internet to conclude that a Samsung would be my best chance to prevent Mo from getting access to it again because I didn't have to log into iCloud. My research indicated that this was the major weakness of the Apple devices for an iCloud email could be cloned. Therefore, I bought myself a cheap Smartphone and buried the other one in Trent Park. I hoped this would be the end of that story. Mo and Brigitta had contacted Josh and Nathalie, and I was therefore afraid that they would try to contact one of my current housemates. It was truly exhausting to be on my guard twenty-four hours a day, but I knew I had no choice but to accept it.

My job had been a contract, and the company ended my employment in January because they didn't have enough work for me anymore. Once again, I had lost everything. Without the little money I received from Universal Credit, I wouldn't have been able to survive. I was in pain; I was angry, and I was broke. In January, I could no longer hear Mo's and Brigitta's voices. With minimal effort, I found out that both of them had succeeded in acquiring a new job. Mo was working for a bank as vice president of sales, and Brigitta had found a job at a social media platform company. I was beside myself. They had tortured me for more than a year, and now they were doing so well. Anger drove me to acquire a new job quickly. After two months, I got an offer from a health and beauty retailer. It was once again a very well-known brand, and I knew it would be great to have that name in my CV. As soon as I thought that, I heard Brigitta say: "Everyone is now going to see Sophie as better than me." At that moment, I knew that the terror was far from being over.

"Oh, do you want me to get rid of her?" Mo asked her.

"Yes, please," Brigitta said in a whining voice.

The words had been spoken to intimidate me. I was fully aware of that. "You are just jealous," I thought. I tried to distract myself with Instagram. There, I saw a post which said: "She is not jealous. She doesn't accept disrespect." I had a bad feeling. Brigitta was now working for a social media platform company. Was she using their software to target me on Instagram? Or had this just been a coincidence?

"So, I disrespect them because I gave out to them because they gained illegal access to my phone and because I sent Mo rude messages because he tried to deceive me. How stupid and ignorant can someone be?" I said out loud. Shortly after, I saw a new Instagram post which said, "If you have to repeat the same thing and their behaviour towards you doesn't change, understand that they don't respect you." "Unreal, they do something illegal and inhuman, and I am, according to them, the one who didn't deserve respect," I thought. I kept browsing through Instagram. Shortly after, I saw a new post which said, 'If someone is not right for you, God will use that person to hurt you until you are strong enough to let go.' I had no more doubts. Brigitta and Mo were targeting me on Instagram, and Mo was using his religion as an excuse to torture me.

On my first day of employment, I had to go into the office to get my laptop. My manager arranged that my team would be there to welcome me. Due to Covid, we were otherwise supposed to work from home. At lunch, we went together to Boxpark Croydon. I realized that I suffered from anxiety and hoped that the others wouldn't realize it. The after-effect of Mo's terror was that I constantly worried that someone was following me, and I was paying attention if anyone said anything suspicious that could indicate that they knew what Mo and Brigitta had done to me. Until two in the afternoon, I was able to think that I was safe in my new work environment.

"He says he will get rid of Sophie. Then there will be more work for me," I heard a girl called Liberty say to another co-worker.

"What are you talking about?" my manager, Darren, asked her.

"I can't believe this. I thought I could go on with my life. Now I have to deal with this terror here as well," I thought. Why did Liberty know Mo, and why did those people think it was ok to do this to a human being? I felt horrible, stressed, worried and anxious afterwards. I had suppressed tears, for it was the most devastating experience and more than anyone could endure. Fortunately, I was able to work from home after the first day. I put all my energy into my work and thought I would gain my co-workers' respect that way.

Most of the designers at the company just did what they were told to do, but I immediately suggested how the website could be improved. In the beginning, it was a fight, but my team realized after a while that the changes I made resulted in higher sales. I felt proud of myself. The success at work gave me somehow the strength to keep going. I had a cooler job than Brigitta and felt like I managed to fight back by being what she feared. Better.

One month after I had started my job, a new head of digital, Paul, joined the company. He was very impressed with me. As a matter of fact, he was so impressed that the management decided to shorten the probation period. After two months, I moved to Croydon, as the office was there. The new room was prettier, and my housemates were nice and respectful, but I wasn't capable of trusting anyone anymore. I kept my phone with me at all times. During working hours, I often heard Mo say, 'I have Sophie see me.' It was very annoying, and it made me think that I maybe was schizophrenic. If Mo could communicate telepathically, I wouldn't have heard the same sentence about twenty times a day. The beginning of the 'telepathic communication', however, suggested unfortunately otherwise.

As soon as the government had declared it was safe to meet in slightly larger groups of people, I decided it was time to get out of the house occasionally. I downloaded the Meetup app and found a Kung Fu class which took place in Battersea Park. I went there every Saturday. It diverted from what I had expected. We often repeated the same movements a hundred times. Afterwards, our teacher, Jo, showed us how to apply those movements in a fight. It reminded me very much of the movie 'The Karate Kid.' During my second lesson, I heard Brigitta's voice again.

"You need to send Zane there. She will kill me," she said.

"But Zane might not win," Mo replied.

"He can shoot her," Brigitta declared.

I was scared. No matter how good I was at fighting, I was certainly not faster than a bullet. I decided, however, that I wouldn't let this threat intimidate me. "If Mo really wanted to kill me, he would have done it already," I thought. It was a mind game, and I was determined to stay strong. Kung Fu training greatly benefited my willpower; it increased my ability to defend myself physically and mentally. Two months later the company decided that it was time that we should work three times a week in the office. At first, I believed that it would improve my mental health to be more around people, but then I had my doubts, for my confidence in my fellow human beings was greatly injured. On the first day back in the office, some of my co-workers asked me if I wanted to join them for lunch. I agreed to it, but then I realized how scared I was to be around people and felt the pain that came with it. Additionally, I recalled that Liberty, who was present at lunch, had said, 'He said he will get rid of Sophie' on my first day of employment. She was acquainted with Mo. I was certain of it and, therefore, had to conclude that she was aware of the cybercrime as well. Naturally, this prevented me from being able to appreciate their company.

A couple of weeks later, I had a one-on-one with my

manager, Darren. We went down to the canteen as it felt more relaxed.

"How are you doing?" he asked.

"I am good. Just tired. I haven't been sleeping very well."

"Have you been drinking again?"

I was too shocked to reply at first.

"No, I haven't."

My conclusion was that Darren must have knowledge of the story with Mo and, therefore, probably as well that Mo had illegal access to my phone. How else would he have known that I once had been drinking too much? I certainly never had told him. The pain nearly tore me apart. My manager, whom I had to work with on a daily basis, was aware that I was illegally spied on and didn't report this crime to the police. It was unbearable. I left the office early that day and got horribly drunk at home. "How would they feel if someone would do this to them? How would they feel if someone would have installed spyware in their phone and could listen to private conversations and even access the camera?" I thought. They had no right to do this. It was very much illegal, and that was for a very good reason. The next morning, just when I had begun to dress myself, the music started playing on its own again. I had enough. Mo wasn't going to cease his mad game, and I knew that I had only two options to put an end to this daily torture. Kill him or kill myself.

I contacted a private investigator to acquire Mo's address, for I was determined to end his life. In order to distract myself, I browsed posts on Instagram. One post said, 'I am actually not really living in a house. I rent an apartment.' "This can't be a coincidence," I thought. To my surprise, I received an email containing the information of his whereabouts by the end of the very same day. I looked up the address on Google Maps. Mo wasn't living in a house as Brigitta had said. He was living in a studio. "Oh, my god. And they said that I was a liar. They are really the most idiotic hypocrites I have had the misfortune to meet. This also proves that Brigitta is really targeting me on Instagram," I thought. After work, I went to Hampstead and took a sharp knife with me, although I hoped I wouldn't need it. I was so angry that I wanted to kill Mo with my bare hands. When I arrived at his place, I felt scared though. It was quite easy to have the thought of killing a human being, but to actually do it was a completely different matter. I banged at his door, but nobody answered.

"It's Sophie. I will send Zane there," I heard Mo say inside my head.

It was impossible to tell whether he was home or not. I waited until ten, but then I realized it was pointless and went home. Mo was always a step ahead of me. He had access to my phone and was, therefore, able to obtain my location whenever he wanted. It felt like he had all the power and, outright control over the situation and my life. It made me furious, and it made me desperate. "If I just would win the lottery. I could hire a hitman to finish Mo of," I thought.

My circumstances forced me to live with the knowledge that my privacy and my mind were violated on a daily basis. The fact that I had to endure everyday emotional abuse without having the possibility to defend myself made me feel hopeless. Alcohol helped me cope with my emotions. I was, however aware that I punished myself for someone else's crime for I was neglecting my health and beauty when I drank and smoked too much. One evening, I watched the movie 'The Pianist.' The movie demonstrated how a person can endure pain, torture, abuse and remain good at heart. It helped me to know that I didn't want to be like Mo and Brigitta, as they were not better than Nazis in my eyes. It was the same principle. They tormented human beings and were convinced they had a right to do so because they believed they had the ability to be superior. Brigitta was well aware that she was not better than me. She had declared so when she said, 'Sophie should not have tried to be better than me.' She was, however, sensible that she could appear superior by destroying me and other women. I hated and despised her but was determined not to sink to her level. She was like the joker from the movie 'The Dark Knight.' She wanted to prove she could take everything from a good human being and turn that person into something ugly. I wasn't going to do her that favour.

In order to remind myself that I wished to remain good at heart, I watched 'The Pianist' several times. I often found excuses to work from home, but I had to go into the office occasionally as I was obliged to. One day, I was very busy at work when I heard Liberty say, 'She watched the pianist again last night.' It was unimaginable cruel. Those people were aware of how much suffering the violation of my privacy was causing me and still didn't stop. They saw my private life as an entertainment show, and it was obvious that my feelings were of no importance to them.

As success was, in general, considered to be the best revenge, I focused on doing well in my job. In order to escape the madness from time to time, I joined a Meetup group in Camden, where I met some fun, kind and down to earth people. Their personalities made me feel welcome and appreciated. One Saturday evening, I was standing outside the Simmons bar with Kaz and Sayed. Kaz was a tall Indian guy and the organizer of the event. Sayed was Pakistani. We were drinking and laughing about some nonsense we had talked about. Suddenly, Sayed took me into his arms. He often did that to show his affection. At that very moment, I saw Mo.

He walked past me and starred at me without any shame. I was outraged, for he showed no fear and no remorse. I noticed again how dark his eyes were.

"Oh, my god," I said.

"What is it, Sophie?" Sayed asked.

"This guy that just walked past us stalked me for several years. We once kissed, but then I rejected him. He cloned my phone and was spying on me to get revenge."

"Do you want to go after him?" Sayed asked.

"I do," I replied, but I couldn't catch up with Mo, for he apparently had taken shelter in another pub or restaurant.

"I didn't know that you can clone a phone," Kaz said when I returned to them.

"I didn't know it either until it happened," I replied.

"Why is he stalking you? That's crazy," Sayed said.

"That's why. He is crazy."

Paul expressed his confidence in my work by giving me two important projects. One assignment involved the design of the brand guidelines, and the other assignment implied the creation of a design concept for a major premium beauty brand the company wished to acquire. I was very eager to perform well and loved working on those projects, for they pleasantly distracted me. Paul thought it would be a good idea to present two concepts to the premium beauty supplier. Therefore, he asked me and the new senior designer, Jolyon, to create one concept each. The day before the pitch, we had a meeting to go over the presentations.

"I think Jolyon's concept is more suitable for the company. It aligns more with what we already have displayed on the website," Paul said.

"The supplier has the right to choose the concept they prefer," I replied.

"They have," he replied.

The next morning, I was very nervous. I practised the presentation in my head in order to feel more confident.

"They want to persuade them to take my concept. So, if you could support me, that would be great," Jolyon told another designer within my earshot.

I was appalled. The premium beauty pitch had been my assignment from the start, and now Paul wanted to influence the supplier's decision. Although Jolyon's words had intimidated me, I was confident that my concept was superior. Jolyon presented his concept first, and then it was my turn.

"Thank you for showing us those two concepts. The second concept is the one we would like to proceed with," a premium beauty brand team member concluded.

My happiness was reflected in my smile. "Eat this, Paul," I thought. Paul's displease was reflected in his facial expression.

"It's just that the first concept is something we usually

would do," Paul said.

I saw the faces of every single member of the premium beauty team. They were very taken aback. "How stupid can someone be? They didn't want to join the company because the current website is not premium enough, and now, he is telling them the first concept is something the company usually would do," I thought.

"The second concept is the one that we want and how we would like to be represented," another member of the premium beauty team said very firmly.

"OK, but it will be a combination of the two concepts," Paul added.

They didn't answer. I could see that not one member of the premium beauty team was impressed by Paul's attitude. After the meeting, I told Darren that the supplier had picked my concept.

"Did they know? Congratulations," he replied.

Afterwards, we had a meeting with the rest of the team. Paul asked us to elaborate on what had happened during the concept presentation. Therefore, I told my colleagues that the supplier had decided to proceed with my concept and showed them my design.

"That's actually really great. I wish the entire website could look like this," one female co-worker commented.

"It will be a combination of Sophie's and Jolyon's

concept," Paul said with a smile.

"That's not what they want," I replied.

"We will see," Paul said.

"I need to talk to you," I said to Paul when all my co-workers had left the meeting room.

"No problem," he replied.

"Why did you tell the others that it will be a combination of my and Jolyon's concept? The supplier said explicitly that they wish to proceed with my concept."

"I just wanted to be considerate of Jolyon's feelings."

"They have made their choice. It's their decision and not yours."

"I don't know what all this is about. You should be happy and celebrate," he replied.

Paul was obviously not capable of acting professionally. Therefore, I concluded that it was pointless to keep arguing with him. On the way home, I bought myself a lot of gin and tonic cans. I sat in front of my house, drank and smoked. My new housemate Arthur came out.

"How did your presentation go?" he asked.

I told him the basics of what had happened. I left certain things out because I was ashamed because the people in my life treated me so badly.

"At least they picked your concept."

"Yeah, it's great."

We talked a little while longer, and then I went back into my room and drank some more. I thought about the events of the day. The supplier had picked my concept. This should have been cause for celebration, but Paul had ruined my moment of glory when he made it evident that Jolyon's feelings were far more important to him than mine. "Maybe that's why I feel so bad. It's like my feelings don't matter to anyone."

CHAPTER 25

A week later, Paul told me that he wanted to exclude me from a meeting with the premium beauty supplier and insisted that Jolyon would be involved to some degree in the project. It was too much for me. I had acquired a twenty-million-pound deal for the company, and was now treated with contempt. I told Paul that I no longer wanted to work with him and handed in my resignation the very same day, fully aware that I never even would receive a bonus for the success I had brought the company. As I was close to burnout, I worked from home and only managed to get through the day by consuming a lot of alcohol. I often cried in the mornings and during working hours but refused to include Jolyon in the premium beauty project. It had been my success, and Paul wouldn't take that away from me.

In my last week of employment, I had a mental

breakdown for Mo's and Brigitta's psycho terror had finally destroyed my spirit. So long, I had battled against them, but I no longer considered my life as something worth fighting for. Paul's behaviour made me believe that no matter what I did and how successful I was, people would never treat me with respect and appreciation. Therefore, I bought two packs of painkillers and swallowed them all, but the suicide attempt failed again. The next day, I called in sick and went into the A&E. A nurse immediately took some blood tests for thirty-two painkillers that could have caused damage to the liver. A little while later, a doctor came to see me. She asked me what had happened. I told her everything that had occurred between me and Mo. The doctor looked beyond shocked when I had finished my story.

"This is so wrong," she replied.

"So wrong certainly doesn't describe the horror I went through," I thought. I started crying hysterically.

"What is it, Sophie?" the doctor asked.

I didn't reply. "What is it? Didn't you hear what I just told you? Why are humans incapable of understanding how horrible this feels," I thought.

"Keep an eye on her. She went through something truly terrible," the doctor instructed the nurse.

It took some time for my tears to dry.

"Can I bring something to eat?" the male nurse asked after

a while.

"Maybe later. I would like to go out for a smoke," I replied.

"Give me a second. I go and get my cigarettes," he said.

As I was suicidal, I wasn't allowed to go by myself. Therefore, I waited and then followed him outside.

"I just wanted to let you know that I believe you. My mother is a narcissist. I know she is because she always tried to control me. I know, therefore, that there are some sick, controlling people in this world," he said after we both had lighted our cigarettes.

"So, you think that Mo and Brigitta are narcissists?" I asked.

"No, I think you met two psychopaths. Sometimes one psychopath meets another, and they make each other stronger," he replied.

"My luck. Meeting two psychopaths. Where are the odds in that one?" I replied.

He laughed.

"I know. You were very unlucky," he said.

Talking to him made me feel a bit better. Probably because he seemed to understand to a certain degree how I felt. Two hours later, a psychiatrist came to see me, and I had to repeat the entire story. I described Mo's behaviour in the office as well. The example of Mo kicking open the door was particularly effective in demonstrating his character.

"Why was he not made redundant?" the psychiatrist asked.

"Someone told me that he was very good at this job, and that's why they didn't fire him."

"That's shocking," she replied.

"So, what do you think?" I asked.

"You probably really met a psychopath. Did you report him to the police?"

"I did, but for them, the evidence wasn't sufficient. Do you think that you could talk to them and tell them that I am suicidal and that they should investigate this?"

"We might be able to do that, but my main concern is your safety now."

"If you could talk to the police, that would really help me. I feel nowhere really safe anymore. I don't know who he might contact or what else he is capable of doing."

"I understand that. I have to talk to my superior and see what we can do to help you."

The thought that she might be able to tell the police that they have to conduct an investigation made me feel hopeful. Three hours later, the psychiatrist came back. She said that they would transfer me to the Home Treatment team. When I asked if she would be able to talk to the police, she answered that they were not able to do that. I fell into despair.

"Do you really think that the Home Treatment team will be able to help me? I need this story to end, and the story will only end when Mo is in jail."

"You can go to the police tomorrow. Just tell them what you told us."

"I have already done that. For them, the evidence not was sufficient, and I am not able to get more evidence without doing something illegal myself."

"I am sorry. Please continue with the Home Treatment team. They will be able to support you."

"Well, thanks," I replied without being able to keep the anger and frustration out of my voice.

Once I was medically cleared, they sent me home. Just when I walked past Big Bang, I heard Mo.

"Yeah, I am really dangerous," he said.

"You are a cold-hearted, insane monster," I thought.

The next day, I wrote Darren an email. I told him that I was sick and, therefore, unable to attend work. The home treatment team came later in the afternoon. They asked me a couple of questions and said that one of their psychiatrists would have to talk to me in order to prescribe medications. Two psychiatrists visited me the next day. I elaborated on everything which had occurred since I had met Mo. I also informed them that I was hearing Mo's and Brigitta's voices in my head.

"Do you think this could be real? Do you think it's possible that someone could communicate telepathically?" I asked.

"No, I do not believe that this is possible. I believe the trauma caused a psychosis," he replied.

I wasn't convinced as I knew the entire story, which had been hard to explain in fifteen minutes.

"We will prescribe you medications, which should stop the voices in your head."

The very same day, someone from the Home Treatment team brought the drugs. The pills made me sleepy, but I still heard Mo's and Brigitta's voices. The Home Treatment team visited me every day for two weeks. During that time, I applied for jobs and soon got a very high-paid offer. As soon as I started working, I heard Brigitta say, "All Sophie can do is sit at home and work. She doesn't have a life." The medications obviously didn't have the promised effect. I didn't enjoy my new job and therefore resigned after one month. The story was never ending, and I was no longer able to see a way out. I drank every day and took one pain killer overdose after the next, for I was determined to end my life.

Every suicide attempt I had made had been unsuccessful. I realised, therefore, that if I really wanted to kill myself, I would have to jump from a cliff. On a sunny day, I took the train to Brighton. As I was aware that I wouldn't have the courage to jump sober, I first went into the pub and ordered two gin and tonics. Tipsy, I took the bus to the cliff. When I arrived at my destination, I had my doubts. "I can't believe it. I am suicidal because of Mo. I promised myself that I wouldn't let him destroy me. Now look at me. When I end my life now, he will have won, and everything I have fought for will have been in vain," I thought. I sat down on the grass at the edge of the cliff, but when I looked down, I felt fearful. At that moment, I knew that I didn't really want to die. I wanted to end the pain, the daily torture, the madness of this impossible situation. "If the police would have investigated Mo, I wouldn't be in this situation now. I really don't understand this system. How is someone supposed to get evidence for a cybercrime legally? Because they didn't do their job, I have taken, I don't know how many painkiller overdoses," I thought on the journey to Croydon. Back home, I met Arthur on the balcony. I told him that I was suicidal.

"I was thinking along the same way. But don't do it."

"I want to do it. I want to end my life. I just don't know how. I went to Brighton today because I wanted to jump off the cliff, but I didn't have the courage to do it."

"Yeah, it is scary when you look down."

"It is. The worst part is that you might survive," I replied. "Do you know how I could get poison?" I asked when he didn't reply.

"You could take rat poison, but it would be a very painful death," Arthur said.

"How come?"

"You would bleed internally for a couple of days until you die."

"Sounds horrible."

"It is. Please don't do it," he replied.

Although I didn't really want to die, I was no longer able to deal with the pain and anger inside of me. Back in my room, I tried once more to cut my wrist with a razor blade. It was not nearly sharp enough to go through. I couldn't live anymore, and I couldn't kill myself. In the hope that someone would help me, I screamed out loud. After my fourth suicide attempt, Arthur called my sister Piera. I had given him her number in case I would succeed. Arthur and I had talked a lot in the last couple of weeks. He considered me as a friend and I considered him the same. It was obvious that he was very worried about me. Shortly after Arthur had ended the phone conversation with my sister, my phone rang. I wasn't happy about it, but I accepted my sister's call. She told me that Arthur had called her to inform her about my constant attempts to kill myself. Piera let me know that she had told Arthur that she didn't really have time but that he had insisted that she would talk to me in order to prevent me from harming myself further. I wasn't able to comprehend why she would tell me something like this in a moment like this. Apart from that, I needed help no matter from which source.

"We will try to organize a place in a mental health hospital in Switzerland for you. Get some rest and try to eat something," she said.

"OK, will do. Thanks," I replied and hung up the phone.

"I can't believe what I have become," I thought while lying in bed. My beauty was gone. My skin was dry and red from the alcohol and the painkiller overdoses. I couldn't get one cheerful thought anymore. My ambition to become a very successful designer was no longer existent, and I certainly was no longer able to hope that I one day would have a romantic relationship. "I am a ship wreck deep down in the ocean. Rusted, useless and hidden behind an ocean of tears," I thought.

The next day, it became obvious that it would be too complicated to go back to Switzerland. It would have taken months to organize a place in a mental health hospital, therefore, I had no choice but to go to the A&E again. I took an Uber to St. Thomas Hospital and brought a bag with me, as I was determined that they would admit me this time. It was the same all over again. A nurse came to see me to take some blood tests. Afterwards, I had to wait for hours until I was able to see a doctor just to tell them the same story once more.

It was so unfair that I was in this situation and that Mo and Brigitta wouldn't face the consequences for their illegal actions. I wanted help so that one day, I would be able to get justice. The psychiatrist wanted to send me home again and proceed with the Home Treatment team, but I insisted that they would admit me. I knew I wouldn't be able to heal from this nightmare at home. Additionally, I was in urgent need of talking therapy to process the trauma.

"You will hate the mental health hospital. You will beg to go home after one week," the doctor said.

"Why?" I asked.

"Well, it's really loud and noisy for a start. You won't get much rest there."

"Right, the Home Treatment team wasn't able to help. Therefore, I think you must admit me. Otherwise, I will try to take my life until I succeed."

"Fine, you might need to wait a long time, though. It's very difficult to get a bed in a mental health hospital."

In the middle of the night, a nurse came to visit me and told me how lucky I was that a bed had become available in the Bethlem Royal Hospital. An ambulance came and picked me up fifteen minutes later.

It was still dark when I arrived at the hospital. "Mo clearly won. He has destroyed my life. Look where I have ended up," I thought as soon as I stepped out of the ambulance. Despite my despair, I knew my strength and therefore hoped that one day I would be able to bring Mo to justice. "I just need to stay alive long enough to take my revenge," I concluded. Once we had entered the building, a male nurse walked towards me to greet me. I was led into the office, for he had to check my bags. He took everything from me that would have enabled me to harm myself or someone else. Afterwards, I was shown to my room, which contained only a small bed, a very uncomfortable-looking blanket and a tiny closet. I couldn't believe it. I was a patient in a mental health hospital. Tears poured down my cheeks once the nurse had left the room. I had tried to be so strong for so long, for I had been determined not to let them win, but after five years of terror, they had broken me. I wasn't ashamed, for I knew it was a miracle that I had survived that horror story for so long. Most people would not have survived if they would have been in my position. "Yeah, everybody said that if this happened to them, they would be devastated. But nobody tried to help," I thought furiously. At half past seven, someone knocked at my door.

"Breakfast is ready," the nurse said.

I usually never ate breakfast, but as I wasn't able to smoke anymore, I helped myself to some scrambled eggs, bacon and toast. It did me good, but I was very bored afterwards and asked myself how I would be able to heal in that place. For me, the only benefit of staying in a mental health hospital was that I couldn't smoke, or drink and that I got three warm meals a day. My skin started to heal, but my mind didn't. Later in the evening, I watched a movie in the common room. A woman played music, and I couldn't hear a word.

"Could you turn the damn music down? Some of us would like to watch the movie," I said to her.

"I do what the hell I want. You bitch."

"What did you just call me? You are rude, selfish and stupid."

She kept quiet, but I heard her talking about me outside the common room after dinner. I had enough. "I am sick of letting people treat me with disrespect," I thought. I took a plastic cup of water, went outside, and threw it at her. She was in a wheelchair and, therefore couldn't defend herself.

"Are you crazy to attack a woman in a wheelchair," she screamed.

"I only asked you to turn the music down, and now you try to bully me and bring other people up against me. Mess with me one more time, and you will face the consequences."

"You wouldn't stand a chance."

"I did Kung Fu and Karate. I would take all of you down in a heartbeat."

A nurse came and put an end to it. He took me into a room and asked me what had happened.

"She tried to bully me just because I told her to turn the music down," I said.

"That was wrong of her. I will talk to her and tell her that she can't do that, but you will have to stay in your room tonight. We don't want the situation to escalate."

I did as I was told and felt good for the first time in a long time. The experience had been liberating, for I had stood up for myself. I had endured daily torture from Mo and Brigitta, but I never had been able to defend myself or punish them for hurting me. The next day, I heard people say that they were scared of me. They greeted me very friendly and didn't dare to gossip about me anymore. Fear was apparently a powerful weapon. I talked once a day with my therapist, Bianca. Talking about the story with Mo and the situation with my family was not entirely useless, but my thoughts were too dark to allow me to heal. Mo and Brigitta had taken everything away from me, including my career, my ability to trust people, and most importantly, my peace of mind. The hate inside my heart tore me apart, for I wasn't able to forget, and I certainly wasn't able to forgive. One evening, I started crying and couldn't stop crying. A nurse came and talked to me. I told her about everything Mo had done to me.

"Now I can't be happy about anything anymore. I just

want to die," I ended.

"How long have you felt that way," the nurse asked.

"For about a year now," I replied.

"Sophie is crazy. They should put her on section," I heard Brigitta say.

"So, I am crazy because I am suicidal, and you are sane, although you stalked me, harassed me and tortured me for more than three years," I thought.

The next day, everything was covered in snow. I wasn't excited, and I wasn't happy. The first snow of the year had always been something magical for me. Now, it was just frozen rain in my eyes. Mo and Brigitta had taken away my ability to feel happy and excited. There was no life left in me, and once I realized that, I was determined to end my life. I browsed through Instagram to distract myself. One post said, 'Did someone ever fuck you up that much that you can't be happy anymore.' By the look of it, Brigitta was proud of herself because she had succeeded in rendering me suicidal.

"How are you doing?" my therapist Bianca asked me the next day.

"I want to die," I told her, for I saw no use in lying.

"Do you think that there is anything or anyone that could you stop to commit suicide," she asked.

"No, there is nobody that I love and nobody that I care about anymore. Nothing in this world can make me stop feeling like I do."

"Really? Nobody that you would be concerned about? Nobody that would be devastated about your death?"

"Nobody," I replied.

Two days later, I told them that I wanted to go home. Three days later, after I had assured a psychiatrist that I was no longer suicidal, I was released. On the way home, I bought myself some beers to celebrate my regained freedom. After I had dropped my luggage into my room, I went out for a smoke. Arthur was sitting on the ground of the balcony with a bottle of wine in his hand. He looked up when he saw me.

"Welcome back," he said.

"Thanks," I replied.

"How was it?" he asked while looking curiously at me.

"It was ok."

"Are you still suicidal?"

"Right now, I am not," I replied truthfully.

I had insisted on going home with the intention of ending my life, but I realized that I didn't want to die. I wanted someone to care about me.

"Good."

He stood up and gave me a hug.

"I am so happy that you are back," he said.

This made me feel so much better. Arthur and I became really good friends after that. We watched movies together, went for walks, and sometimes just talked for hours. The day before Christmas, we went to Greenwich. It was the most beautiful place in London I had ever seen, and the view from the park was just spectacular. I was determined that one day, I would live there. On Christmas, I cooked a beautiful dinner for Arthur and myself. The steak was absolutely perfect, and even Artur said so. We watched the entire evening of Christmas movies. It was nothing special, but after all that pain I had experienced, it felt special to me. Arthur, who had a serious drinking problem, ceased consuming alcohol for a while, and so did I. He became better, and I became better. My savings however started to run out, and the support I got from Universal Credit wasn't enough. I was panicking because I worried about how I would be able to pay the rent. Arthur went on a holiday to Poland, and when he came back, he started drinking again. I encountered him at seven in the morning with a bottle of whisky in his hand. Of course, I tried to help him for a while, but he was an alcoholic as it stood in the book and could, therefore, not be reasoned with. It became obvious that our friendship neither benefited him nor me. Therefore, I was once more on my own. "Why do I have to be always alone and go through so much heartache?" I asked myself.

One month later, I got an offer for a position as a user interface designer. The job was very high paid, and I knew that with the salary the company would pay me, I could afford my apartment. The manager, whose name was also Darren, was so nice to me. I had great hopes that I finally had found the place where I belonged. Shortly after I had commenced my new job, it became obvious that I would have to deal with annoying and disrespectful people at the workplace again. I had to show some of my designs to Levan, who worked in the marketing team. He did not understand graphic design or design principles but wanted to play a wannabe. Once, he even laughed about my designs. I was furious, but as Levan was a really good friend of the marketing director Vato, I wasn't able to say anything. Some aspects of my job were enjoyable, and therefore, I stayed. I got really high praise for the redesign of the website and other user interface projects. Just after one month of working at the company, I heard Brigitta again.

"Everyone will see Sophie as better than me," she said.

"Do you want me to get rid of her?" Mo asked.

"Yes, please," Brigitta replied.

"Not this shit again. Why can't they leave me alone?" I thought. I felt fearful and angry for still having them in my head, and my devices meant that I wasn't able to heal or to proceed with my life. "How am I ever supposed to have a social life when their terror keeps stressing me out?" I asked myself. "They have made it impossible for me to enjoy any aspect of my life," I thought furiously. The anger was so bad that my muscles painfully contracted. In order to relieve the tension, I consumed alcohol again. I heard stuff like, "I will fire her." I wasn't sure whether it had been Mo's or Darren's voice. There had been indications that there was something wrong with Darren as well. I once had a chat with him on the balcony, and then he slammed the balcony door five times. He had reminded me very much of Mo in that moment. I was confused because I didn't know what was real and what wasn't anymore.

One month later, I got the news that my grandfather's second wife had died. As my grandfather and my mother both were dead, me and my sister would inherit the money. I knew the inheritance would provide me with some security for a long time. On a Thursday, Darren told me that the new sportsbook I had designed for them was so good that they wanted to sell it as a template. The next day, Darren informed me that he and the product owner had made design decisions without me. I couldn't cope with hearing voices and the stress at work. Additionally, Darren's behaviour had reminded me of Paul and the trauma I had experienced when Paul had tried to influence the supplier's decision. Therefore, I handed in my resignation.

Three weeks after I had quit my job, I moved into my apartment in Greenwich. For the first time in a long time, I was free of worries and toxic people. At least I was able to think that for a day. As I needed a lot of stuff for my apartment, I went to IKEA the day after I had moved in. The shopping was fun, and I listened to music to make it even more enjoyable.

"Sophie has moved out. Now everyone will see her as better than me," Brigitta said just after I had selected a plant for my apartment.

Suddenly, the music I was listening to on Spotify played fast forward. I did restart my phone, but it happened again. Mo succeeded in ruining one more experience, which could have been really fun without his terror.

CHAPTER 26

I signed up for BetterHelp, a mental health platform providing online services. The first therapist, which had been assigned to me, was horrible. As soon as I told her the story with Mo, she told me she wouldn't be the right person to treat me. "Unreal, as it is not bad enough that I had to go through this horror story, and now I don't even find a therapist that wants to help me heal from this trauma," I thought. After two days of sulking, I decided to give another therapist a chance, who turned out to be great. I told her everything Mo had done and said during my time at CooperateEvent and described thoroughly what had happened to my phone. She believed me, and she also declared that Mo was most likely a psychopath. The fact that he had slammed the computer mouse on the table and kicked open the office doors was enough for her to make that diagnosis.

It didn't really soothe me at all, for I had recounted Mo's anger outbursts to the police as well and also informed them that there had been cameras all over the office. The recordings of Mo's violent behaviour would have provided some form of evidence after all. In regards to the voices in my head, she only said that certain things indicated that there was a possibility that Mo and Brigitta had found a way to communicate telepathically. Still, she wasn't sure, and I wasn't sure either. After the second week of therapy, I had an outburst of rage in my apartment. I couldn't forgive, and I certainly couldn't forget. Therapy alone was clearly not enough to process those traumatic events. Mo and Brigitta had destroyed every aspect of my life and every single moment that could have been enjoyable without their interference. It was unbearable that they were walking free despite the horrendous crime they had committed. I screamed in my room and said that I would kill them. It was an empty threat, but sometimes the anger was so intense that I thought I could really do it. I browsed again through Instagram posts. Just minutes after I shouted, I saw the post again, which said, 'If you have to repeat the same thing and their behaviour towards you doesn't change, understand that they don't respect you.' I was so angry that I needed to go to the shop and get myself a beer so that I was able to calm down. It had not been a coincidence. I had seen that post every time I had shouted in my room. Brigitta was targeting me with the software from the company she worked for. I kept browsing through Instagram. I should have stopped, but I couldn't. Then I saw again the post that said, "Did someone ever fuck you up that much that you can't be happy anymore.' I screamed out loud, for the pain and anger were unbearable.

The next morning, I woke up with the idea of writing a novel. I wanted to tell the truth and, at the same time, find answers to questions. When had Mo cloned my phone? How had Mo and Brigitta been able to reaccess my phone after I had changed it? Were they able to communicate telepathically, and could they hear my thoughts? Or had the trauma really caused a psychosis? Did certain events trigger this psychosis? I was determined to make sense of everything that had occurred.

I told my therapist that I wanted to write a book. She approved and said that it would be very therapeutic for me. Although the story with Mo was fascinating, she wanted to discuss my childhood as well. I told her that my father had hit me a couple of times and that he had told me that he had to be mean to me because the world would be mean to me.

"Was your father abusive towards you?" she asked.

"I don't know. How would you describe it?" I asked.

"He was abusive. He was emotionally and sometimes physically abusive. He degraded you to destroy your self-esteem. He isolated you to make himself look good, and you look bad. It's hard to believe that a father would do that to his child. Therefore, it is important to understand the narcissistic personality disorder," she replied.

I told her that I sometimes had anger outbursts as a kid.

"You had anger outbursts because you were abused. You knew that your father's behaviour was intended to destroy your confidence. You only defended yourself. By the sound of it, your father has a narcissistic personality disorder. He didn't care how you would feel. He cared how he could make himself feel good. Making you angry was certainly a tool to achieve that."

"It's really hard to accept that I had to go through so much rubbish in life because of my father. It makes me angry, and it makes me sad."

"Most people who experienced trauma in their childhood suffer severely in their adult life. When you are loved and well taken care of in your childhood, you will grow into a well-functioning adult. Someone who was abused in their childhood will always have to deal with the effects of the maltreatment. This may involve anxiety, anger, problems with trust, self-destructive behaviour, depression and substance abuse," she said.

"Makes sense. I often experienced intense anger and definitely always had problems trusting people. I was afraid I would be bullied again wherever I went."

"It certainly is a lot to process, and it will be challenging to overcome all those traumatic events, but with talking therapy, we will be able to make good progress."

I knew she was right and became aware that I probably had attracted Mo and Brigitta to my life because of unresolved childhood traumas.

After I had written about forty pages of my novel, I typed in 'Bahrain people' into Google, for it was important to understand Mo's origin. I browsed through the images my search had brought up. One image of people protesting in Bahrain caught my interest. I clicked on the image. The article's headline was 'Unsafe anywhere: women human rights defenders speak out about Pegasus attacks.' The article pointed out that the Pegasus spyware was able to gain access to a device and extract data, including text messages, emails, media, passwords, voice calls on messaging apps, location data, call logs and contacts. Pegasus enabled the attacker as well to activate the phone camera and microphone. Particularly intriguing was the information that the attacker had complete control over the victim's device. This included control over the music app, which explained how Mo had been able to play and change the music on my iPhone as he pleased.

The spyware was used in Bahrain to repress human rights defenders, activists, journalists and even lawyers. Pegasus was described as a powerful weapon utilized to intimidate, harass, and publicly smear the targets' reputations. The article provided two examples which demonstrated the harm that had been done to the victims of the Pegasus attacks. After I had carefully examined the article, I conducted more research on the Pegasus spyware. Particularly interesting was the information that Pegasus was capable of infecting a device without the user needing to do anything. The term used for it was a zero-click attack. An example of a zero-click attack was when the victim received an unknown call. Although the owner of the phone didn't accept the call, the phone was still infected with the Pegasus spyware. Another form of attack was the delivery of an iMessage. Often, an iMessage was sent, which informed the owner of the phone that a parcel hadn't been delivered and that a reschedule of the delivery was required. The earliest version of the spyware required the target to click on a malicious link in a text message or email. In 2020, the creator of the spyware, the NSO Group, enabled the zero-click attack. Therefore, only the phone number or an email address was needed to infect an iPhone or Android phone with the Pegasus spyware.

After about twenty minutes of doing research on the

Pegasus spyware, I looked through my iMessages. One message had been sent from a mobile number. It said: "EVRI: If you don't reschedule a new delivery date, your parcel will be sent back to the sender." I hadn't given the message much consideration before, but everything made sense at that moment. Additionally, I remembered all the weird calls I had received since I had met Mo. He had infected my phone with the Pegasus spyware. I was certain of it. It clarified how he had been able to access every phone I had purchased since the first attack. It explained why he had been driving by Nathalie's house at the precise moment when I had been outside for a smoke. He had been able to see what I had been doing twenty-four hours a day.

The minding reading and the voices inside my head were still a mystery. Therefore, I conducted more research. In one YouTube video, it was mentioned that the Pegasus spyware was able to access thoughts. They didn't elaborate on that point, but I assumed that the reason for that was that people concerned didn't dare to speak about it, for they were afraid of being labelled as crazy. At that moment, I recalled that Nathalie had been concerned that I could have heard Josh say, 'This is incredible,' while he had the headphones on. I could, therefore only assume that Pegasus enabled the person in possession of the spyware to listen to the thoughts of the person whose device had been infected. Therefore, I conducted more research. Apple had published a screenshot of the Pegasus spyware interface.

In the navigation bar was a button called telemetry. My investigation made evident that telemetry uses infrared, ultrasound and radio waves. Infrared is capable of measuring the blood flow to the different areas of the brain. Infrared, in combination with artificial intelligence, makes it possible to interpret someone's thoughts. Every smartphone uses NoFeb magnets. Those magnets, in combination with radio waves, which are part of telemetry, make it possible to send a message to someone's brain. Many companies have been working on mind-reading technologies and have now succeeded. I could, therefore only conclude that Pegasus was way ahead of the other companies. Neurable had been working on a headphone with sensors embedded in them. AI interprets the information collected from those sensors. Infrared renders those sensors, however, as unnecessary.

I remembered that Mo had followed me when I had been dating Tim. He only had been able to do that by knowing my location, and he had only been able to access my location with the Pegasus spyware. "But how on earth had Mo been able to infect my phone with the Pegasus spyware? He didn't have my number," I was asking myself. "No, he didn't, but Vince had it. Remember? He asked you to exchange phone numbers after you heard him say 'I can't do that'," a voice in my head said.

Mo and Brigitta claimed that they had done this because I had sent Mo some rude messages on Teams and lied to Mo. The truth was that they had done this because I had rejected Mo and because I had declared that the violence and abuse inflicted on victims in certain Muslim countries, especially in the United Arab Emirates, was wrong. For Mo, I had been a threat from the moment we had met. I had not been someone he had been able to manipulate with his charm. I had been someone who had rightfully guessed what kind of person he really was. Mo had never been able to recognize that his actions were wrong. The way he had looked at me when he had walked past me in Camden had demonstrated this. He had gazed at me without fear and remorse.

Mo had not been able to see anything wrong with his actions because Bahrain had a long history of human rights violations. My research made evident that the NSO group sold the Pegasus spyware to countries such as Bahrain fully aware that the spyware could be abused to harass, torture and intimidate innocent people who posed a threat to their beliefs and their desire to oppress.

It became evident how easy it must have been for Mo to discredit me by making use of the Pegasus spyware. Mo had been able to see and made public everything I had done, including, for example, my abuse of alcohol in the moments of despair. The people involved in the cybercrime hadn't been able to comprehend the reason for the alcohol consumption or anger outbursts. They only had seen my reaction to the abuse. I was also certain that he had recorded me when I had had intercourse with Dimitri, and Mo had used that recording to shame me publicly. "God, he should be hanged for this crime," I thought once I realized what he had done.

The aftermath of the Pegasus spyware was a severe form of post-traumatic stress disorder. The victims, which included me, lived in a perpetual state of fear and became socially isolated and restricted in their social lives and work. Additionally, the victim of a Pegasus attack often felt so hopeless that, at some point, they wanted to end their own life. I concluded, therefore, that it was safe to say that Mo's abuse of the Pegasus spyware was equal to attempted murder.

Further research provided me with the information that LULU, a Pegasus operator that was attributed with high confidence to the government of Bahrain, had hacked four human rights activists. After all my research, I no longer considered Mo as a psychopath. His culture had taught him that abuse of that nature was acceptable. Brigitta was a woman of no beauty who sought to raise her self-esteem by destroying the life of another woman. Many people had said that Brigitta was one of the ugliest women they had ever seen.

Therefore, I had always asked myself why Mo was with that woman.

That mystery was finally solved. Mo had learned in his childhood that abuse was acceptable and tolerated. Brigitta, who suffered most likely from a narcissistic personality disorder, had indorsed Mo that abusing people was not only justifiable but also desirable. I was sure that Mo appreciated that as he didn't wish to think that anything his parents or country did was wrong. Most people would label a woman who asks her boyfriend to see other women as a bitch, for it is cruel to deceive and humiliate another person like this. Brigitta, however, was apparently not able to see anything wrong with her actions. In her head, she believed that she was entitled to be superior even when that meant to destroy the life of someone innocent.

The Pegasus spyware hadn't been invented, as the NSO group had claimed, to investigate terrorists. They had developed the spyware because it provided unlimited power. Power over other human beings. The abuse of the spyware was evident with several well-known examples, in particular in Bahrain, where women, journalists and lawyers were tortured and shamed because they fought for human rights.

Yusuf Al-Jamir, for example, was in two thousand eleven questioned and harassed by the Bahrain government for he worked as a protest organizer. He was detained multiple times and faced several episodes of alleged torture, assault, interrogations and rape threats by the Bahraini intelligence agency. In two thousand seventeen, he moved to the United Kingdom. In 2022, Al-Jamir alleged Bahrain's government of hacking his phone with Pegasus. Legal filings suggested that he had been infected with Pegasus in 2019. What a coincidence, for it was the same year that I noticed someone had control over my phone.

"You are right, Brigitta. We all should see you as better because you support and encourage this kind of abuse and human rights violation," I thought, furious and sarcastically.

What agitated me was that many people had known that Mo had infected my phone with the Pegasus spyware, but nobody had reported him to the police. The people who had participated in Mo's cybercrime allowed, therefore, that the abuse and mental torture, executed in countries like Bahrain, took place in the United Kingdom. Human nature always had aimed for power. History has taught us this much. The best-known example was, of course, the Second World War, which demonstrated that an entire country could be persuaded to kill, torture and abuse in order to be considered superior.

Further research demonstrated that over forty countries had already purchased the Pegasus spyware. It was very concerning when I considered in what way the Pegasus spyware had already been abused and asked myself the question of what consequences it would have for mankind, especially when I considered that idiots like Mo and Brigitta were in the possession of the most powerful spyware that had ever been developed. The day after I had done most of my research, I went for a walk in the park. I was furious and simply couldn't believe what Mo had done.

"Sophie lied to me," I heard Mo say.

"Yes, and she paid the price for it," Brigitta added.

According to them, telling a lie was reason enough to use a spyware that had been developed to spy on terrorists. It wasn't even surprising anymore because in the United Arab Emirates anyone, who asked for freedom of speech, was considered a terrorist, according to Ghanem, a Saudi comic living in London. Apart from that, Brigitta's argument that they had done it because I had told a lie was ridiculous. "Mo could not have known that I told a lie without the Pegasus spyware."

CHAPTER 27

My research had certainly been illuminating but not comforting. If Mo had my email addresses and phone number, he most certainly could gain access to my devices whenever he wanted to and no matter how many times I changed them. Even if I had moved to another country or even continent, he would have been able to access my contact details, one way or the other, again. It was scary, devastating and infuriating at the same time, for it was nearly impossible to detect the Pegasus spyware and to prove the cybercrime for the Pegasus spyware was equipped with a self-destruct mode and the possibility to erase any traces of it with one command.

This meant that I could have tried to prove that my phone had been infected with the Pegasus spyware and that Mo would have been able to eliminate any traces of it at precisely that moment. Afterwards, he would be able to install the Pegasus spyware again. It was so brutal, that I didn't know if I would ever be able to have a relationship with a human being again.

My faith in humanity was shattered. The revelation made me paranoid, for I looked constantly over my shoulder to see if I was being followed and listened to the conversations of my surroundings in order to investigate if they were talking about me. Mo wasn't able to live with my rejection of him, and he probably was aware that his relationship with Brigitta could only be considered as a joke. After all, they stalked someone twenty-four hours a day. What kind of love was that?

Brigitta had no other way to raise her self-esteem but to try to destroy mine. Brigitta had asked Mo to see me because she had not been able to accept that the people at CooperateEvent could have potentially considered me as more beautiful than her. I remembered that she and Mo had been driving by Nathalie's house. I had been sitting outside and had taken a photograph of myself when I heard Brigitta say, 'She just took a selfie to show me that she is way more beautiful than me.' What kind of logic was that? She had gained illegal access to my phone and had felt less of a person because I had taken an image of myself. It had been obvious that Brigitta was a very stupid person with no morals from the beginning. It was shocking, especially when I considered that Dumb and Dumber, also known as Mo and Brigitta, had been able to manipulate people. "What is the average IQ of a human being when someone as stupid as Brigitta is able to influence other people's opinion of someone?"

The question was why this had happened to me and if a happy ending was possible. Then I remembered a beautiful line from the movie 'Batman Begins.' 'Revenge is about making yourself feel better. Justice is about creating harmony.' For the first time in my life, I understood those words. If I had killed Mo and Brigitta, I would have gotten revenge, but never justice.

The Pegasus spyware was a global threat, and good and innocent people were the victims. Additionally, many people got bullied in their lives. Bullying can be a devastating experience, for it is hurtful when you realize that so many people group up to bring you down. Some kids don't even want to go to school anymore because they get cyberbullied, and in the worst case, a victim of bullying becomes suicidal.

I was convinced that my novel was the answer to achieving justice by demonstrating to the victims of the Pegasus attacks and victims of other forms of abuse and bullying that they were not alone. I wanted to give them hope, implying that the worst could be endured and their freedom and happiness could be regained. Furthermore, I wanted to give them the tools to heal from their trauma and to turn the anger and pain into success.

The people who had participated in the cybercrime may have thought that they had shamed the victim, but in reality, they had shamed themselves. They had taken part in something truly evil, and had to live with that guilt for the rest of their lives. Their harassing actions were disgusting and could only be regarded as disgraceful. Although the victims of the Pegasus attack and bullying, which included me, had suffered severely, they remained good in nature. I considered that something to hold on to and that I hoped I would never forget.

If I would have retaliated, I would not have been better than Mo and Brigitta. For me, those were pathetic, power-hungry fools who spend their time stalking and harassing instead of living their lives. They probably claimed they had found true love, but what kind of love was that? Or was stalking someone the new form of romance? Those kinds of people were definitely not worth it to commit a crime.

I thought a lot about the people who had supported Mo and Brigitta. Those people had been able to hurt me in the past, but then I asked myself what the people who would read my novel would think about Mo's supporters. What would my readers think of someone who helped a woman who asked her boyfriend to sleep with other women and to harass them when they didn't want him? Most people would think that Mo's supporters are ignorant fools who tried to distract themselves from their pathetic life by hurting and harassing someone.

I wanted my readers to remember that. Those people only participated in bullying because they were bored and frustrated with their own lives. It still did hurt, but I expressed my pain by writing about it. By doing so, I saw clearly, and by doing so, I healed.

The worst consequence of the Pegasus attack was that the victim felt hopeless and thought they didn't have a way out because the zero-click attack made it impossible to defend themselves against Pegasus. Those kinds of feelings could result in an attempt to kill themselves and potentially in a successful suicide. I was determined to find a way out, and I was determined to demonstrate that healing from any form of abuse was possible. Of course, I informed my therapist about my discovery, for talking about it was an important tool to get better.

"That is shocking, and it is scary," she replied.

"It most certainly is. I think that people underestimate the threat of advancing technologies. A software like the Pegasus spyware should not be allowed. Additionally, I am angry because the police should have investigated Mo. Any cybercrime claims should be taken seriously and inquired into immediately by the relevant authorities. I think that a lot of changes are necessary, and I hope that my novel will demonstrate that new technologies are required to identify a spyware early in order for the police to be able to conduct an investigation.

Additionally, any knowledge of a cybercrime of that nature should be reported to the police at once. Any person who doesn't notify the relevant authorities is equally responsible for the consequences of the Pegasus spyware attack on the victim. The person who abuses the spyware should be held accountable for their crime and receive the appropriate prison sentence."

"You are right. Absolutely right," she replied. "How do you feel now?"

"I am angry. I am so angry that sometimes my muscles contract painfully."

"What do you think is a good way to deal with that anger?"

"Writing about it certainly helps. It's an outlet, but sometimes I need a drink to calm myself."

"What could you do instead of having a drink?"

"Well, I could release my anger by hitting on a punching bag," I replied.

"That certainly is a good idea."

The journey of writing and editing the novel was

liberating, illuminating and empowering. Of course, it wasn't always easy. Some memories were so painful that my tears were flowing like an ocean, but every time I edited a particular traumatic chapter, I healed. I hoped that my novel would give other victims of abuse hope, inspiration and guidance. In order to achieve that, I first had to heal from my traumas, and therefore, I had to discuss my childhood and the treatment I had received from my family with my therapist.

"I think we need to talk more about my family because I am angry because of the maltreatment I received from my father, and I am angry because my sister supported my father instead of me," I said to her in a therapy session.

"Why do you think your sister has supported your father?" she asked.

"I think a child wants to love its parent. No matter what. My father gave life to my sister. He provided for her, paid for her education and was definitely nicer to her than he ever was to me. She didn't and doesn't want to accept that he was abusive towards me and that he severely traumatized me because if she would, then she would have to think ill of him. She doesn't want that because he is her father, and she wants to love him."

"I think you are absolutely right. The way you are able to analyse someone's behaviour demonstrates that you are very intelligent," she said. "Do you miss your sister?"

"No, just because we are bonded by blood doesn't mean we are connected. I think the only people you should bond yourself to are the people that make you feel good about yourself. Otherwise, you won't be able to love yourself," I replied.

"Do you love yourself now?" she asked.

"I struggled to love myself my entire life. My family made me believe that there was something wrong with me because I reacted angrily several times. Now I realise that my anger has always been justified. There is something wrong with the abuser and not with me. The answer to your question is, therefore, yes. I love myself now. I realized that I didn't deserve the ill-treatment I received during my life, and I am proud of myself that I managed to stay a good and decent person despite all the crap that happened to me."

"You really can be proud of yourself. You had to endure a lot of suffering, but you learned from it, and instead of letting the pain destroy you became stronger."

Although I made good progress in the therapy sessions, I realized that it would take longer than I wanted to heal from all the trauma truly. For example, I walked once in Greenwich, and someone laughed while passing me.

"Is this person laughing about me? Does he know Mo, and has he seen all that Mo has been able to capture with the

Pegasus spyware? I asked myself. I talked with my therapist about it.

"You were triggered, and it's important to identify those triggers and find a good response to them," she said.

"How exactly am I supposed to do that?"

"For one thing, you can ask yourself if there is anything ridiculous about you."

"There isn't anything ridiculous about me. Quite the opposite. I am strong, brave and intelligent. Mo is ridiculous. He is a real idiot who just happened to acquire the most powerful spyware of all time."

"There you are then. You can deal with those triggers by knowing who you are and reminding yourself of all your good qualities."

I did as she told me to. It was a real effort, but I found it a lot easier to respond more confidently to those triggers after a while. The anger, however was a real problem. Brigitta and Mo had damaged my life. Their terror had overshadowed my success as a graphic designer. Every relationship I had since I had met Mo had been destroyed because Brigitta had been jealous. I realized that anger was like drinking poison and expecting them to die. Forgiveness was the only way to be truly free and truly heal. Not because they deserved my forgiveness but because I deserved to be happy.

CHAPTER 28

I worked really hard on the manuscript. After six months of writing and editing, I was finally happy with it. I sent the manuscript to a handful of literary agents. For two weeks, I waited. It was agony, for I saw the novel as my only chance to achieve justice and to regain my freedom. I wanted to show the world what kind of people Mo and Brigitta really were, and I wanted to help victims of abuse to heal from their trauma. I wanted to believe that this had happened to me because I had the strength to endure it and because I had the skills to make a difference in this world, but after I had sent the manuscript, it was out of my hands and the decision laid with people who knew what would sell and what wouldn't. I was confident that my novel was great, but it was my first novel, so I couldn't be sure. Three weeks before Christmas, I finally got an email from an agent.

Hi, Sophie,

I read your manuscript and think it is really special.

The story is interesting, informative, heartbreaking and inspiring.

I am more than happy to submit your manuscript to publishers, which I think would be suitable. Leave it up to me.

Merry Christmas and a Happy New Year,

Regards,

George

The waiting time was tough. Although I had succeeded in acquiring an agent, I was still not sure if the book really would be published. I always loved animals, and as I had money and time, I bought myself a puppy. She got the name Bella. From the moment I saw her, I loved her like I had never loved anything before. I only wanted to make her happy, protect, and care for her. For the first time in a long time, I was able to feel joy again. "This is love," I thought. Humans often seek confirmation about their worth from other people. Once I got Bella, I realized I didn't need a human being to be happy. "Nobody wants to be alone, and therefore, we often attach ourselves to toxic people, especially when we experienced abuse in childhood," I concluded. Still, I was no longer alone, and all the abuse I had to endure didn't change who I was. I was a good, kind, loving, caring woman, and Bella reminded me of that.

I was so busy caring for Bella that I didn't even think about my novel. On a January morning, I heard back from George.

> Hi, Sophie,
>
> I hope you had a lovely Christmas.
>
> Great news. Three major publishers want to make an offer. The advance they are willing to pay demonstrates what a huge potential your manuscript has to become a bestseller novel. Therefore, I think we should go to auction.
>
> Please let me know your thoughts.
>
> Regards,
>
> George

George had attached a Word document with a list of the publishers that wanted to make an offer and the advance they were willing to pay. I opened the document and looked at the numbers. For a minute, I thought something was wrong with my laptop or my eyes. I had never expected to receive such a high advance offer. As a matter of fact, I had googled before what the average book advance for a debut novelist was. My research provided the information that the standard advance was less than six thousand pounds. Therefore, I couldn't believe it.

> Hi, George,
>
> Happy New Year.
>
> Thank you so much for your email. I can't tell you how delighted I am.
>
> Did you make a mistake in the Word document? I mean, did you add a zero too much?
>
> Regards,
>
> Sophie

I got a response fifteen minutes later. George confirmed that the numbers were correct. "Oh, my god. I can't believe this. My book will get published, and the advances they are willing to pay are so high. Eat this, Brigitta," I thought. Two weeks later, a publishing deal with HarperCollins was made. I insisted prior to signing the contract that I would design the cover myself. Every company I had worked for had profited from my design skills, and now it was my turn to receive finally the credit I deserved. Of course, there was still a lot of work to do on the manuscript. I didn't really agree with every editorial suggestion, but HarperCollins had a good reputation, so I decided to trust my publisher. HarperCollins was convinced that my book would become an international bestseller, and therefore, their team suggested selling it to a film production company before the launch. Two months later, we got an offer, which was jaw-dropping. "Ha, Brigitta has succeeded in humiliating me in an entire city. I succeeded to show the entire world what a crazy, cruel, pathetic bitch she is. What concerns Mo is that he will regret the day he heard about the Pegasus spyware," I thought.

Four weeks before the release, I received a copy of my book. The feeling I had when I looked at it was hard to describe. I had not only survived a horror story but also succeeded in turning the pain I had experienced into a success and a tool to help millions of people to heal from abuse, humiliation and failure by demonstrating to them how I had mended my mental health. In the first week after the release, it became apparent why the publisher had dug so deep with their advance offer. I was so happy, but more rewarding were the comments I saw online.

"I was bullied as a child and suffered my entire life from social anxiety. Your book showed me how to turn pain and anger into triumphs. Thank you so much for sharing this story," read one.

"My father was abusive. I could very much relate. Your book showed me that I am not alone and inspired me to process my childhood trauma," read another one.

"The revelation about the Pegasus spyware and what it can do to a human being is shocking. We should all protest to ensure that this spyware will be banned," another one wrote.

These comments made me feel better than the money I earned with my book, for there had been a purpose in my pain. I was helping and inspiring people. It was such a triumph. Brigitta and Mo failed to destroy my life and turned me into a better human being than I ever thought I could be.

Three years later, I was late for my therapy session and was, therefore, driving really fast. On the journey to the praxis, I reflected on everything that had happened after my novel had been published.

"Hi, Michelle. Sorry for being late. My baby girl Jane kept me up all night," I said to my therapist when I arrived fifteen minutes late.

"No problem, Sophie. I completely understand," she replied. "How is Jane?" she asked

"She is great. I love her so much," I answered with a huge smile while sitting on the couch.

"I am glad to hear it," she said. "How are you doing apart from not getting enough sleep?"

"I am doing good. Sometimes it's still hard to believe how

much success, money and happiness my novel has brought me and that I am married now and have a five-month-old daughter," I replied.

"I can imagine that," she replied. "The movie came out two weeks ago. How did you feel when you saw it?"

"Honestly, it wasn't easy to see how much suffering Mo and Brigitta caused me, but I was delighted about the ending. I think I really succeeded in inspiring people. Maybe not everyone, but at least I reached some people," I replied.

"I am sure that you did. You have every reason to be proud of yourself. I think what you accomplished exceeded every expectation."

"It did, but for a high price. I have my freedom now because I am rich, but I suffered grievously. I am married now and have a daughter, but no matter what I wrote in the book and what I told the press, I will never forget what Mo and Brigitta did to me."

"No, the story you lived and wrote is unforgettable. But look at how many people you inspired. Look at your ending. You are married and have a daughter and a dog you love. You are rich, which I am sure helps a lot. You got a house in the Hamptons, Aspen and an apartment in London. Of course, money is not the key to happiness, but it certainly helps. Some people would say that your story is a fairy tale instead of a thriller," she replied.

"To a certain degree, it is."

"Then what concerns you?"

"The memories, Mo and Brigitta were so generous to give me will stay with me for the rest of my life. I am sometimes still scared that he will try again to sabotage my life, but in general, I feel confident that even when he would try it, I would be able to handle it."

"How would you handle a new attempt of Mo's to sabotage your life?" she asked.

"Well, Mo has demonstrated the power to abuse the Pegasus spyware and I have demonstrated my power to fight, succeed, heal, and love."

ABOUT THE AUTHOR

Milush Black isn't just an author; she's a storyteller in every sense. Her debut novel, "The Power of Pegasus," is an inspired thriller that will keep you reading all night. Her characters are multi-layered and her plots are gripping.

Printed in Great Britain
by Amazon

42626656R00189